Flippers, Blades and Murder
Apple Creek R-Parks Department Mysteries
Book 1

Montie Red

This book is a work of fiction. Names, characters, places and incidents are either product of the author's imagination or are used fictitiously. Any similarity to actual people (living or dead), events, or locales is entirely coincidental.

COPYRIGHT © 2025 MONTIE RED

All rights Reserved. No part of this book may be reproduced, scanned, distributed, or used in any printed, electronic, digital or any other form without the express permission of the author. Please do not participated in or encourage piracy.

ISBN: 978-1-962293-04-4

Editing by First Editing

Cover design: MRed

Map Illustrator: M Red

Library of Congress

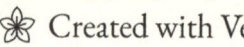 Created with Vellum

To my biggest and most interesting mystery in life, Josephine

Chapter 1

"For the ten-thousandth time, Mom, it's called Recreation and Parks, not Park and Rec. That's your show," I said, raising my voice and exhaling in frustration. It was exasperating that not even my mother could get this detail right.

"But it's the same thing, isn't it?" Mom said as she poured steaming water into an old blue cup with a line of flowers at the bottom.

I shook my head, overwhelmed by memories of her past attempts to cheer me up. During my college years, I had always yearned to come back home. But now, standing in the kitchen where so much felt familiar, I was plagued with doubt. Why did it all seem so scary now?

I let myself sink into the wooden chair by

the window and traced the old scratches on the kitchen table. Mom set the cup in front of me and moved closer.

"You really shouldn't have scratched my table this much," she said. But when I looked up, her sad smile lit up her face—a look I desperately didn't want to see.

"I'm fine, Mom," I said quickly. "Just look at you. You got through Ben's breakup, and you're doing great. We'll be fine. Darcy and I will rebuild our home here.

Mom's expression froze, and I immediately regretted mentioning Chief Morales. My dad had passed away before I was born, and my mom waited over twenty years to date someone new. Ben was a part of our lives for almost a decade before the breakup.

"Well, Ben and Andrew made their choices," she said, walking back to the table with her own cup in hand. "Eventually, you'll look back fondly on your time with him and be ready for what comes next."

I smiled faintly, but a nagging worry lingered. How was she really coping after five years alone? I didn't question her breakup with Ben. Maybe she wasn't questioning Andrew's departure because of that. If I asked why she'd stayed alone all those years, she might ask about my choices, and I wasn't ready to go there.

"And, I'm sure Darcy will love it here, pretty," Mom said as she sat down across from me. "But she's five. No matter where she is, living with her grandmother will make her world rock."

I chuckled and took a sip of the tea. It tasted just like I remembered—the sweetness of honey and the freshness of mint. Somehow, it made everything feel a little better.

"You mean rock her world, Mom."

"Same thing," she said, waving her hand dismissively and taking a sip of her tea. "And my point stands. She'll be fine. I'm more worried about my baby."

She patted my hand, looking at me intently. I wasn't ready to dive into my personal life, but I did have a professional problem—and Mom always gave the best advice.

"The Recreation and Parks Department? It's a big job, Mom," I admitted. "Running a natural resources program is one thing, but managing an entire department? I have no idea where to start."

Mom leaned back, cradling her cup in both hands with a proud smile on her face.

"There's a reason they hired you, Maggie.

They believe in you. And I know you can do it."

I smiled back, but not because I felt confident. I didn't want to explain that I'd been the only applicant—they hadn't had much choice. Just thinking about walking into the office the next morning made my heart pound. Not for the first time, I wished Darcy's father hadn't taken that job on the other side of the world.

I had known I didn't want to marry him, even when I was pregnant. A long-distance relationship wasn't an option either. And he'd proved me right when he packed his bags, promising to send money and call Darcy weekly.

"Everything will be all right," Mom said, patting my hand again and pulling me out of my thoughts. "You need to rest and relax. It was a long road trip, and tomorrow will be a big day for the Willow girls."

I raised an eyebrow and leaned closer. "I know what I'm doing tomorrow, but what are the other two Willow girls up to?"

"Three," Mom corrected me. Before I could protest, she continued, "Your sister is taking Darcy and me shopping."

"Shopping? Mom, Darcy doesn't need—"

"She needs to make that room feel like

Flippers, Blades and Murder

hers," Mom said, grinning. "And you are not going to stop our fun. You go and play in your parks."

I rolled my eyes. Even though Darcy couldn't wait to start kindergarten and live with her grandmother and seemed okay with her dad's new job—better than I was, honestly—I knew she missed more than just him after we moved away from the city.

Chapter 2

"Mrs. Willow," a man wearing a shirt and tie, met me by the main doors of City Hall, the old Roman-looking building on Main Street. His round face held a pleased smile and an unmistakable air of self-satisfaction. "It's so nice to meet you. This position has been open for a few months, and your impressive resume makes you the perfect candidate."

I reached for his hand, and his grip was so strong I swore I heard my fingers crack before he let go. "Thanks. I'm sorry, I don't know who—"

"Of course! I'm just so excited you're here. I'm Norman Beltran, and starting today, I'm back as the Operations Maintenance Manager."

"Today?"

His smile somehow spread even wider. "Well, I don't have to run R-Parks—sorry, the Recreation and Parks Department—anymore. Back to business, which, if you can't tell, makes me really happy."

I chuckled and nodded, though inside, my stomach flipped over.

"Let me show you around, Mrs. Willow."

"Miss Willow, but please just call me Margaret," I corrected him, trying not to make a fuss.

His face flushed red and his cheerful expression faltered.

"I'm so sorry. I didn't mean—I should've reread your résumé this morning, but I remember you have a little girl and assumed—"

"It's not a big deal," I interrupted him, just as mortified as he was. "Like I said, Margaret is fine."

He inhaled deeply, squared his shoulders, but his earlier enthusiasm remained slightly dimmed. "Miss Willow," he said loudly—too loudly. A few people at the front desk turned to stare. "I mean, Margaret. It won't happen again. Promise."

"Oh, it will happen again," said a deep and unmistakable voice from behind me. My stomach did a little flip as butterflies woke up in it. Even if I'd wanted to pretend I didn't recognize him, the bright smile and overconfident eyes of my old high school classmate forced a grin onto my face.

But it wasn't Logan's smile that brightened my day—it was the brown, long-eared dog sitting obediently at his side. Seeing the K9 vest on the playful puppy I'd met years ago filled me with pride, even if it was the only thing keeping me from crouching down to pet him.

"Come on," Norman said, unfazed by Logan's joke. "Miss—Margaret, this is Officer—"

"Logan Forest," I interrupted, watching Norman's mouth fall open. "Though I can't believe you're a detective now. And with such a wonderful partner, too."

Logan chuckled and dramatically pushed his jacket back, resting his hands on his hips to ensure I noticed the shiny badge clipped to his belt. "Come on, Maggie. I was a great student. Never as good as you, but I wasn't a troublemaker. Not like this one down here."

"Bruno is an angel!"

This time, both men turned to look at me in surprise, while Bruno let out a shy whine.

"How do you—Chief Morales!" Logan exclaimed. "Of course you've met this piece of work." He gave Bruno's head an affectionate pat. "He's on probation these days," Logan added with a wink.

I crossed my arms, ready to defend Bruno's honor, but Norman interrupted before I could.

"So, you two know each other?" Norman asked, his eyes full of sincere confusion. "I thought you just moved into town?"

"That's a fair question," Logan said, narrowing his eyes in mock seriousness. "I didn't know you were coming into my office today."

I stared at Logan for a moment before deciding it was best to ignore him.

Our paths had crossed many times. Logan had been in my sister's class, a year ahead of me, and he used to date my sister's best friend. His best friend, meanwhile, had been my sister's boyfriend. So, unless I counted *the* incident during spring break—an incident I tried not to think about—we were just acquaintances. *Good* acquaintances.

"You're correct, Norman," I said finally. "I just moved here from the city, but I grew up in Apple Creek."

Norman nodded, back in good spirits. "Got it. Well, in that case, our tour should be easier. You'll be familiar with our parks."

I felt my anxiety spike. The last thing I wanted was to appear as if I already knew everything about my new job. This was heading in a direction I didn't like.

"Don't be so sure, Norman," Logan said, stepping forward—a huge mistake. Bruno immediately took the movement as an invitation to launch himself at me. Standing on two legs, he licked my face enthusiastically.

"Hey, buddy," I said, rubbing his face and scratching his ears. "I missed you, too! Look how big you are now!"

"Bruno!" Logan shouted, pulling the dog back down and tightening his leash. He scowled at me, though his tone was more resigned than angry. "You're not helping him."

Logan sighed and shook his head. "Anyway, Norman, Maggie hasn't been around in years. I'm sure she'll need a tour to see all the cool changes in town."

"Of course," Norman agreed. "I wouldn't know where to start if I went back to my hometown."

I couldn't confirm if Logan realized how much his words had eased my nerves and if Bruno's antics had been a deliberate distraction. But when Logan winked as he walked past, I found it suspicious.

"I'll see you at the meeting tonight," Logan said to Norman, his voice casual.

Bruno's tail wagged a mile a minute as he trotted off beside Logan, his fur shaking with every step and stealing a smile from me. Logan clearly misinterpreted it because he called over his shoulder, "Margaret, it was very nice to see you."

I was grateful Bruno pulled him away before he could see the blush spreading across my cheeks. Thankfully, Norman was too distracted to notice, either.

"And this is where the magic happens," Norman said as he opened the last door on the third floor of City Hall for me.

The sounds of people chatting and typing reached me, but we were interrupted before I could step inside.

"Mr. Beltran!" a loud voice called from behind.

I turned just as a tall, broad-shouldered woman emerged from the elevator and strode toward us. She wore bright red and yellow sweatpants with a matching shirt—an outfit impossible to ignore.

"I'm waiting for your reply to my concerns," she announced, glaring at Norman.

"Mrs. Taylor," Norman said, stepping forward with a polite but measured tone. "We're working as fast as we can to accommodate your—"

"You and your people are doing *nothing*!" she shouted even louder, stopping so close that I couldn't help but notice her overly smooth skin—thanks to heavy makeup—and her fake, super-long eyelashes. Her chic short haircut couldn't disguise the fact that she was closer in age to my mother than to me. *"I sent that request a week ago. Is this what you want me reporting to the Charter Commission?"*

Norman took a measured breath before replying, "Of course not, but the email was sent just yesterday. Sunday."

"Are you correcting me?" Her hands flew to her hips as she bounced slightly on her heels. *"I won't hesitate to get you fired. As Chair of the Commission, I can do it. This city has overlooked my people for far too long."* She turned abruptly and stormed down the hallway.

"I'll wait inside," I told Norman softly.

"Thanks, Margaret," he said, rushing after

Mrs. Taylor. I silently prayed I would never cross paths with that woman again.

City Hall was an old building—full of charm but not without its limitations. Each department was tucked into large sections spread across the floors. The first floor housed public affairs, Council Chambers, and a few meeting rooms. The police station sat next door, with internal access to this building. The second floor was reserved for council operations and city development planning. Finally, the third floor housed Finances, Human Rights, and R-Parks.

Recreation and Parks sat at the far end of the third floor. While it meant a longer walk, the trade-off was worth it: more windows and a better view—a beautiful sight of my hometown.

Inside the department, desks were clustered into small modules, and I spotted a larger meeting room with a long table, along with two closed offices.

I had barely stepped inside when Norman's voice startled me from behind. My heart nearly leapt out of my chest. I guessed it was good he was back, but I wished he'd been a little noisier. Surely everyone had seen me jump.

"Morning, everyone!" he called, easily grabbing the room's attention. I just hoped no one noticed my knees shaking or my palms sweating. *"I want you all to welcome our new R-Parks director."*

He paused, glancing at me. Logan's earlier warning about Norman's memory flashed through my mind.

"Margaret," I whispered.

Norman visibly relaxed, shoving his hands into his pockets and nearly bouncing on his heels. *"Margaret,"* he repeated. *"Let me introduce you to the team."*

The surrounding faces turned to me, some curious, others smiling. This was the part I dreaded the most—getting to know the people I was supposed to manage. In my old job, there were only two other employees, and we never discussed who was technically *in charge*. Being a boss was new to me, and I was clueless about my role.

"Team, this is Mrs.—Miss—Margaret, your new boss."

I laughed nervously, more from my own jitters than the moment itself. A few people chuckled too, lightening the mood.

"All right," Norman said, heading for the door. "They're all yours. Have a great day, Margaret."

I watched him leave, the door closing behind him. A childish urge to run after him flickered through my mind, but the silence that followed forced me to turn back and face my new team.

"Well," I began, clearing my throat, "I suppose Norman isn't great with names."

Thankfully, everyone laughed at my weak attempt at humor, and I felt the tension in the room ease a little. Just as I started to breathe easier, the door burst open behind me, making me *jump* again.

"I'm so sorry, Miss Willow," said a man with graying, unruly hair and an askew tie. He extended his hand, which I shook automatically. *"The mayor had some questions regarding our engagement program, and I couldn't get here earlier. I hope Norman showed you around? I'm Martin Norton, the city manager."*

"Nice to meet you, Mr. Norton," I said, nerves flaring up again as I realized I was now shaking the hand of my *new boss*.

"Martin, please. I feel old enough already." He grinned but didn't wait for me to respond. *"Now, let's make a proper introduction to your team."*

I turned to follow him, and to my surprise, everyone had already gone back to work. I hoped that was a good sign. Martin had sounded perfectly reasonable during my phone interview, but aside from that, I didn't know him well. I guessed I'd just have to wait and see.

"Good morning, Linda," Martin said to the woman sitting at the first desk. "I want you to meet our new director. I'm sure she'll help resolve many of the issues you've been handling over the past year. Margaret, this is Linda Oak, the department's secretary."

Linda smiled warmly at me, and I wondered if my mom might have known her through one of her friends. Between Linda's oversized sweater and worn sandals, it was clear she'd been part of this office for a long time.

"It's very nice to have a new director around," she said in a raspy but kind voice. "We really need some direction here. And there's a ton of paperwork to go over and sign. I'm glad you're here."

Martin nodded, and though I managed a smile, my stomach churned. "Well, I'll do my best."

"That's awesome!" A short man with a

funny, bouncing walk approached Linda's desk. "We need to make sure the council pays attention to our projects instead of just passing us by."

Martin sighed as the man extended his hand to me. "Margaret, this is Bert Smith. He's the department's facilities manager and your—"

"Best ally!" Bert interrupted, grinning, which prompted Martin to shake his head in exasperation.

"You'll see, Margaret," Bert said with a mischievous twinkle in his eye. "When you deal with these wannabe important people, you need someone at your side."

"Bert," Martin said, his tone more weary than stern, "we've talked about this. You can't refer to the council like that."

"Who says I was talking about the council?" Bert raised his hands in mock surrender, though his grin suggested otherwise. "Lots of people want to be important people."

Linda muffled a laugh as Bert turned and called over his shoulder while walking away. "I look forward to chatting with you. Lots of facilities in this town need improvement—like yesterday!"

Martin sighed again before refocusing on

me. "Bert is one of the younger members of the team. He's talented but... lacks patience. You'll need patience to work with the city."

He didn't wait for my response and moved toward a closed office door. After knocking only once, he pushed it open. I was immediately struck by the sheer number of boxes and piles of paper crammed into the small space.

"Tara, are you here?" Martin called, weaving his way inside.

A large hair bun emerged from behind a computer monitor, followed by wide, startled eyes.

"Oh, boy!" Tara exclaimed, springing up from her chair. A few boxes teetered precariously, and some papers slid to the floor.

Martin crouched to pick them up, but Tara beat him to it, kicking the fallen sheets under her desk. "Not important," she said with a sheepish, apologetic smile. "I'll print new ones, anyway. Hi, I'm Tara Jones."

She extended her hand but quickly withdrew it, wiped it on her shirt, and offered it again. "Sorry. I was wrangling with the printer."

I shook her hand, glancing at the ink stain now smudged along the seam of her shirt.

Tara followed my gaze and waved dismissively. "It was bound to happen," she said with a shrug. "It's my connection to my inner child."

I laughed, feeling an immediate connection with her. "Once I've had my first coffee, I'll be right with you."

Martin cleared his throat, bringing us back to the moment. "As you can see, Tara stays busy. She runs the recreational programs."

"Tries to run them," Tara corrected with a grin. I couldn't help but notice Martin shifting his weight, crossing and uncrossing his arms, before finally shoving his hands into his pockets.

"Well," he continued, "she does a fantastic job, and the city is extremely thankful. Without Tara, the kids wouldn't have any activities."

Tara's face lit up, and she fidgeted slightly, her smile growing wider. I pretended not to notice their mutual awkwardness. "I'm sure you're doing an incredible job. Maybe a little help will—"

"Oh yes!" Tara cut in enthusiastically. "Help would be very much appreciated."

A sudden crash outside interrupted us, and Martin hurried out of the office.

"Who put that garbage can there?" a voice demanded. A man about my age, sporting an elaborate hairstyle and an overly fancy suit for City Hall, stood amidst the commotion.

An older man with a clumsy step and a rounded belly rushed forward, his expression worried.

"Oh, I'm sorry, Rufus. Let me help you with—"

"You know what, Terry?" the man called Rufus interrupted sharply, his tone cutting. "The less you touch, the better. I don't need anything else misplaced, and you're not exactly known for your competence."

"Rufus," Martin interjected, his voice firm. Both men turned toward him.

Terry looked genuinely apologetic, but Rufus met Martin's gaze with an air of smug superiority.

"Terry was just trying to help," Martin said evenly.

"It'd be better if he didn't create problems in the first place," Rufus retorted.

I didn't like Rufus's tone—or his attitude. My opinion of him sank further when I realized the garbage can he'd bumped into was bolted to a heavy cabinet. Anyone paying attention would've noticed it. I said nothing, though, and crouched to pick up a flower vase and a picture frame from the mess. The photo inside showed a young girl about Darcy's age hugging Terry.

Linda appeared beside me, silently helping to gather Terry's scattered belongings.

"Oh, dear," Terry murmured as I handed him the frame. "Thank you. I don't have many pictures of my granddaughter." He smiled wistfully before adding, "But, oh boy, this isn't how I wanted to meet our new director."

"Well, it'd be a miracle if you didn't mess something up while meeting her," Rufus said, shoving Terry aside to step in front of me.

"I'm Rufus Taylor, the Assistant Director of Community Outreach and President of the Youth Advisory Committee."

Chapter 3

"He really said that?" my sister, Sandie, asked, leaning on the kitchen counter while I warmed up my leftovers.

"Yes, and his tone wasn't any less arrogant either," I said, stirring the food on my plate, not bothering to sit at the table. "But he wasn't the worst part of my day."

Sandie tilted her head and stole a potato from my plate.

"Hey! You already ate!"

"I'm eating for two here."

I rolled my eyes. Sandie was expecting her second baby, but being pregnant wasn't strange to me. That was simply a pretext for enjoying Mom's famous creamy potatoes.

"Well, go on," Sandie said, taking a sip of her water. "What happened?"

"The council meeting happened." I shook my head and stared at my plate. "I really messed that one up. But in my defense, I had no idea there was a meeting tonight, or that I had to stay, let alone talk."

Sandie frowned. "You? Messing up a meeting? This I've got to hear."

I took a deep breath as the memory of the embarrassment came flooding back.

"After meeting everyone, I spent most of the day learning about projects and sites I'd never even heard of before," I said. "Then, I found out I had to stay for an *off-schedule* meeting that lasted two and a half hours. By six o'clock, my brain was already dead."

Sandie chuckled, stealing another potato with a wicked smile. "Did you yell at the mayor? Or better yet, did you tell him to shut up?"

I tried to swat her hand with my fork, but she was too fast. "Of course not! But I did call him Henry right after he asked me his first question."

Sandie placed a hand on her heart, pretending to gasp. "Oh, no! Did you dare to use his first name?" She chuckled again and leaned forward. "Wait, that's not his name?"

"Sandie! You don't even know the mayor's name?"

She shrugged, unconcerned by my genuinely exasperated tone. "Who cares? All he does is plan holiday events and cut ribbons."

I rolled my eyes, resisting the urge to lecture her about the importance of local elections and city leadership. "His name is Henry Dosal. The problem is, I'm supposed to call him Mister Mayor whenever I address him."

For a moment, Sandie just stared at me with wide eyes. Just as I thought she might understand my frustration, she burst into laughter.

"What did you—" she tried to ask, but her laughter got the best of her.

"Shh! Sandie, you're going to wake Darcy and Mom."

She raised her hands in mock surrender, struggling to breathe between giggles. By the time I was almost done with my dinner, she'd finally managed to calm herself.

"Sorry, Maggie," she said, wiping her eyes. "But you can't honestly expect me to believe this is a huge issue."

"Well, the mayor wasn't thrilled about correcting me," I said, rinsing my plate in the sink. "And of course, I had no idea what he was asking about. He hated me for not knowing the data he wanted."

Sandie smirked. "Sounds like a 'him' problem."

"Maybe, but it only got worse from there. One of the council members, Raymond Hudson, used my mistake to attack the mayor and the project he was asking about. The whole meeting turned into a chaotic shouting match." I shook my head. "This council is something."

"That much, I know. But nobody listens to Hudson. Don't worry about him—or the mayor."

"That's nice of you to say," I replied. "But it'd be more convincing if you knew anything about the city."

"What's that supposed to mean?" Sandie asked, raising her voice. "Everyone in Apple Creek knows Hudson is disgusting!"

I crossed my arms and raised an eyebrow, waiting for her to elaborate.

"He used to be on the school board," she said. "I know Toby was in kindergarten that year, but my neighbor is always talking about how he nearly destroyed the schools with his cheap decisions."

"You and your neighbor know Hudson, but not the mayor?"

Sandie grinned. "She's a teacher. And she threw a party when he moved off the board."

I chuckled and shook my head. "Well, the meeting went on and on, with everyone shouting over each other. Honestly, I would've been concerned, but the police chief didn't seem bothered—or surprised."

Sandie clapped her hands. "See? Nothing to worry about. You didn't ruin the mayor's chances for re-election."

I groaned, covering my face with my hands. "I hadn't even thought about that."

"Maggie, do you *really* think the mayor disliked you just because you didn't use his title?" Sandie asked, voicing the same question I'd asked myself after the meeting.

"That was my initial thought, but then Logan told me it wasn't my fault."

Sandie, who had been heading for the couch, froze. She turned to me with her hands on her hips and a deep frown.

"Logan, the traitor, Forest?"

I rolled my eyes at the unfair nickname she

and her best friend had given him years ago. Even after too many other ex-boyfriends.

"You talked to that human and didn't lead with that?" Sandie added when I didn't respond.

"I was busy complaining about my day."

"And when exactly during your horrible day did Forest show up? Because I know I would've noticed his name earlier."

I sighed, knowing there was no way past her, pregnant belly and all.

"I knew you'd get upset. That's why I didn't bring it up earlier."

Sandie shifted her weight and narrowed her eyes. "Upset? That know-it-all broke Lucy's heart. My best friend in the entire world! I'm glad you're ashamed to be talking to him."

I said nothing, but her comment bothered me. I knew that wasn't how things went down between Lucy and Logan, but now wasn't the time to correct her.

"So, Margaret," she continued. "I hope you don't plan on talking to him regularly."

I didn't bother looking at her as I replied. "Hard to avoid when we work in the same building, and some projects involve the police department."

"I live in the same city, and I've never needed his services as an officer."

"That's good. I don't want my big sister getting in trouble with the law. And he's a detective."

Sandie groaned, but finally sat next to me on the couch. I leaned my head on her shoulder, enjoying the quiet moment. Life had changed a lot in the past few months, but being close to my family made the chaos worthwhile.

Chapter 4

Projects, new coworkers, and procedures blurred together as the rest of the week flew by. I probably failed at everything. By Sunday, I was grateful for a day to focus on Darcy and me.

Walking down Main Street, my five-year-old bounced up and down while gripping my hand. Her face lit up at every little detail of my hometown, and her endless stream of questions kept me smiling. Nothing in the world could steal my happiness at that moment.

I started to feel I'd made the right choice by moving back to Apple Creek. I wasn't rushing through errands like I used to in the city, and I was looking forward to walking Darcy to school when summer ended in a few weeks. Mom had offered to help after school, something she was clearly excited about, and Darcy was already warming up to her cousin, Toby. She seemed excited about the coming baby, too.

"Hey, want to check out the bakery before the town's history museum?" I asked.

Darcy's eyes widened, and a huge smile spread across her face. I gestured toward the other side of the street. "When I lived here, my favorites were the blueberry muffins, lemon cookies, or maybe chocolate—"

"Donuts!" she shouted, tugging me toward the road.

"Wait, crazy lady," I said, redirecting her toward the corner. "You can't just cross in the middle of the street. That's dangerous."

"And illegal," came a deep voice behind us, startling me. Darcy, on the other hand, let out a high-pitched squeal and slid behind me, still clutching my hand.

I turned to see Logan, who immediately held up his hands in apology.

"I'm so sorry," he said. "I didn't mean to scare you girls."

His expression was so genuinely concerned that I couldn't help but laugh. Darcy peeked out to inspect him from head to toe.

"I'm sure you weren't sneaking up on us," I said, narrowing my eyes at him playfully.

Logan grinned. "Catching criminals here requires sneaking around."

Darcy gasped softly, her grip tightening on my hand.

"Not that you're a criminal, of course," Logan added quickly, trying to sound less serious, which only made things worse.

I crouched down to Darcy's level. "Sunflower, this is Logan Forest. He's an old classmate of your Aunt Sandie and me."

Darcy gave a shy smile and whispered, "Hi."

Logan crouched too, staying a respectful distance away. "I couldn't help but overhear that you're heading to the bakery. Let me tell you, Sunday mornings are the best time to visit —unless you like the ice cream shop better."

Darcy's eyebrows shot up, and she looked at me with exaggerated hope. "Can we get ice cream, Mommy? Please?"

I brushed a strand of hair from her face, smiling, then shot Logan a mock glare.

"Maybe later, when they open. What about that donut?"

Darcy squealed again, this time with excitement, and bounced on my hand.

"Yes!" Logan exclaimed, clapping his hands together. "But I'm more of a pie guy myself. It's healthier." He winked.

"Healthier?" I raised an eyebrow. "I'm sure the sugar-free vegan crust may qualify as healthy?"

"Exactly," Logan replied, straight-faced. "As long as there's double whipped cream. I need my sugar fix before lunch. Trust me—you don't want to see me without it."

Darcy giggled, and we walked to the bakery door, which Logan held open for us. But just as we stepped inside, his phone buzzed. His face turned serious.

"I have to take this," he said, walking back toward the street.

Darcy tugged my hand. "Is he okay, Mom?"

I nodded but glanced over my shoulder at Logan. Knowing where he worked made my imagination run wild.

Darcy's attention shifted as we reached the bakery counter. She pressed her nose against the glass, staring wide-eyed at the pastries on display. The smell of sugar and coffee beans hit me, and nostalgia warmed my heart. I remembered coming here as a kid, feeling just as excited as Darcy looked now.

"So," I asked, raising my eyebrows at her, "what's it going to be? Cookies or donuts?"

In the end, she picked a delicate pavlova topped with fresh fruit and cream. I had no idea how I'd gone years without trying it. We found a table, and while I waited for my tea and her milkshake, Logan walked back inside.

To be honest, I hadn't expected to see him again that day. He was busy enough as it was, and he didn't owe me any explanations. Still, the moment he spotted us, he made a beeline for our table.

"So," he said, hands in his pockets, "my evil plan was to ambush your morning and invite you two wonderful ladies to breakfast. But I had to check on something."

Darcy, her face covered in sugar, beamed at him but stayed quiet, her mouth too full to speak. I tried to act casual, but Logan's serious tone and quick smile left me unsettled.

"I guess we'll have to get ambushed another time," I said. The second the words left my mouth, my heart skipped a beat.

Logan caught the slip, his smirk unmistakable, but he said nothing—probably for Darcy's sake.

"What's that?" he asked her, pointing to her plate.

"It's a pavlova," she said proudly. "And it's scrumptious."

"Scrumptious?" Logan grinned and looked at me. "How did we miss this one?"

After Logan left, about twenty minutes later, my phone rang. Norman's name lit up the screen. For a moment, I debated answering. It was Sunday, and the week had already been long enough. But my curiosity won out.

"Hello?" I said casually.

"Oh, Margaret, I'm so sorry to bother you on the weekend," Norman began, his voice shaky. "I wish I didn't have to call, but... well, something's happened. Something... unusual."

I straightened in my seat, sensing the tension in his voice. "You're not bothering me. What's going on?"

There was muffled shuffling on the other end, followed by several bumps and a distant voice.

"Norman?" I prompted, my nerves on edge.

"Yes, officer, I understand... just let me—of course."

The noise stopped, and when Norman spoke again, his voice was even more unsteady.

"There's no easy way to say this, so I'll just

say it. Councilmember Raymond Hudson... has been murdered."

My breath caught.

"What?"

"Yes, officer... oh, sorry, Margaret," Norman stammered. "It—it happened in one of our courts. The gymnasium at the community center. I—I think we're under investigation!"

Before I could respond, Logan's voice came through the phone, calm but firm.

"Maggie," he said, his tone setting my nerves on edge. "I need to ask you some questions. Can you come to the community center as soon as possible? I know you're with Darcy, and I hate to interrupt your day."

I looked at Darcy, who was now watching me intently.

"Twenty minutes?" I asked, mentally calculating how quickly I could drop her off at home.

"That'll work," Logan said. "And Maggie? Please keep this between us for now. We can't release a statement yet."

Chapter 5

After seventeen minutes, I was rushing from my car into the Community Center. I hadn't expected to find so many police patrols and officers guarding the place. For a moment, I lost my way amidst the chaos. People bustled through the building's doors while reporters darted around, cameras rolling as they chased anyone who looked like they knew something.

One reporter locked eyes with me. Before I could react, he pointed at a man carrying a large camera, and the two of them sprinted across the parking lot toward me. That snapped me out of my daze. Hurrying toward the main door, I evaded them, but my escape failed when I almost tripped over the yellow crime scene tape I'd missed.

"Only authorized personnel can come in," an officer said as he stopped me short. Before I could reply, Logan appeared from the building.

"She's with me, Joe," he said to the officer, who nodded and lifted the tape.

Logan gestured for me to follow him, and my legs turned to jelly. This wasn't my first brush with a crime scene—Logan had been there during that time, too—but unlike him, I hadn't grown comfortable with such things. He might have become a police detective because of that experience, but for me? I'd vowed never to see another dead body if I could help it.

"We can talk by the rink," Logan said, his voice steady as he led me toward the entrance of the ice arena.

The chill from the refrigeration system greeted me, giving me an excuse to wrap my arms around myself.

"Why am I here, Logan?" I asked, unable to keep the tremor out of my voice.

Logan scanned the rink, even checking the stands to ensure we were alone. When he returned, the concern etched on his face sent fresh waves of anxiety through me.

"Maggie," he began gently, "like Norman told you, Councilmember Hudson is dead—

and it wasn't an accident. I need to ask you—"

My hands flew to my mouth as my chest tightened. I shook my head, struggling to breathe. After a few deep breaths, I found my voice, though it quivered with panic.

"Am I a suspect? I can't be a suspect again! Logan, I didn't hurt anyone. I don't even know him! Before this week, I had no idea who he was! You can't seriously think I—"

Logan took my hands in his, his gaze steady and grounding.

"I would never even consider you a suspect, Maggie," he said, his voice unwavering. "But you are the R-Parks director. I need your help understanding some things."

The warmth of his hands steadied me, even as my nerves buzzed. I fought to push away flickers of memory from our spring break all those years ago.

"I know you just met him," Logan continued, releasing my hands. "This isn't about that. Norman mentioned a project involving the removal of an ice rink to build a pool. Can you explain it?"

My mind, still spinning from the murder and Logan's sudden questions, grasped at the vague memory of something I'd read earlier in the week.

"Sort of," I began. "But it's not a project—it's just a proposal. It's not set in stone. From what I understand, there's resistance from residents, and the department has to provide more information to justify the idea."

Logan nodded, but I noticed his sharp focus hadn't wavered.

"Who's against it?" he asked.

"The hockey associations and the skating school to start," I replied. "They don't want to lose an ice sheet. But the swimming club and some residents have been pushing for an Olympic pool to be built in the city. Other residents are upset about losing an asset, instead of adding options to our programs."

He mulled this over, tapping his index finger against his lips—a gesture I remembered well from years ago. Somehow, the familiarity eased my nerves, though his next question brought them rushing back.

"If it's only a proposal, why are people so upset about it?"

I threw up my hands in frustration. "I have no idea, Logan! I really don't! I've barely started this job. I haven't even had time to dive into it yet."

"It's okay," he blurted, his tone soothing. "I know you just got here. I just need to understand this from the department's perspective."

A creeping concern settled in the back of my mind, and I had to ask.

"What happened to him?"

Logan's expression darkened, and he ran a hand through his hair as he turned away. My stomach sank. Whatever had happened, it was bad.

"Logan?" I prompted.

He turned back to me, hesitating before he answered.

"Someone hit him in the head," Logan said. "With a skate blade."

My breath caught, and I turned to stare at the pristine ice sheet behind me. Too many skates had marked the surface with countless cuts. My stomach churned at the thought of what had happened in the gymnasium just down the hall.

"That's awful," I whispered.

Logan nodded grimly. "I need to see everything you have on this proposal. Norman... well, he's not in the correct mental state to help right now. Can you get me the information?"

I nodded. "Everything should be in my office. I'll go there now and find it. I can meet you afterward."

Logan gave me a small smile. "Sorry to ruin your Sunday."

Before I could respond, he was gone.

The rink fell eerily silent except for the low hum of the cooling system. I saw that not all the lights were on, and the far end of the rink near the Zamboni storage was dark. A flicker of movement near the storage doors caught my eye. For a moment, I thought I saw a shadow slip across the dimly lit space, but when I blinked, it was gone.

I froze, my heart pounding, and stifled a startled gasp.

"Hello?" I called out, my voice trembling. No answer. No further movement. Just the hum of the machinery.

I took a deep breath and hurried out of the rink, the hum of the cooling system lingering in my ears. The unsettling feeling clung to me, crawling up my spine with every step toward my office.

The Community Center and City Hall were on the same block, but at opposite ends. With so many people milling around and sections of the path blocked by police, it took me nearly fifteen minutes to reach the third floor. I rushed down the hallway, my pulse racing.

When I arrived, I was startled to find the office door wide open. Considering what had just happened, my heartbeat quickened, and my nerves went on high alert. I stopped in my tracks, clutching my phone tightly. Peering inside, I called out, "Hello?"

No one answered. Instead, I heard movement from the far end of the department, where the light in the file room was on. Criminals wouldn't bother turning on lights, would they? I stepped inside cautiously, trying not to make a sound.

Halfway across the office, I recognized Linda moving back and forth in the file room. Relief washed over me, though it was short-lived.

"What happened here?" I asked, stepping into the room. Papers and folders were scattered across the floor, and Linda was frantically picking them up.

"Miss Willow—Maggie," she stammered, her tone a mix of frustration and panic. "I have no idea. But all my work—everything—is a mess!"

I crouched down to help her gather the papers, though I wasn't sure if I was putting them in the right place. For Linda, this chaos was unthinkable. In the few days I'd worked with her, her meticulous, over-organized personality had proven to be the backbone of this department.

"This is unacceptable," Linda huffed, shuffling papers with little regard. "I wanted to get ahead for Monday's meeting—my husband's birthday is tomorrow, and I was hoping to leave early. But then I walked in and found this!" She gestured wildly at the room, her hand finally landing on her desk at the far end of the office.

"I know there are missing files, Maggie! And who knows what they did on my computer!"

"Oh, my," I said, moving toward her desk. I hadn't noticed it when I first came in, but now I could see that her workstation was just as messy—papers, office supplies, and personal items strewn everywhere. The other desks and cubicles, however, seemed untouched.

I stepped into my own office, my hands trembling slightly. Everything was exactly as I had left it. A flicker of relief passed through me. "Did you call—?"

"The police? Oh, yes," Linda said, struggling to stand. I hurried over to help her. "I called them the moment I saw the door open, but they haven't shown up yet. And the station is just downstairs! Unbelievable."

Linda had a point. Normally, the police would have come straight up. But today's events had probably thrown everything off.

"You don't know what happened?" I asked, watching her carefully. I hoped her blank expression was from shock, not guilt. "Councilmember Hudson was murdered in the Community Center gym. Sometime today, or maybe last night."

Her face turned ghostly pale, and she suddenly leaned heavily against me, catching me off guard. I barely managed to keep us both upright.

"Hudson is dead?" she whispered, her voice trembling. "I know he could be... difficult... and people didn't like him, but murder?" She looked at me, her eyes searching mine for answers I didn't have. I could only shrug.

"What happened?" she asked as I guided her to a chair.

I hesitated, still shaken myself. The scattered papers and the disarray in the office sent a chill down my spine. This department was supposed to be about recreation and parks—about fostering joy and community. Not... this. I didn't want to let Logan down, but telling the truth seemed like the right thing to do then. And I knew what happened.

"Officer Forest said he was struck in the head. With a skate," I said, keeping it vague but truthful.

"An ice skate?" Linda's voice shot up an octave. Her complexion turned even whiter, and her hands began to shake.

"Linda, are you okay?" I knelt in front of her, afraid she might faint.

She grabbed my hands, gripping them tightly. "Please tell me it was a roller skate."

I shook my head. Her reaction was immediate—she dropped my hands and leaped to her feet, moving to her computer. Her words came out in a frantic mutter as she powered it on.

"I knew this proposal would cause trouble. But this? I never imagined... We're a peaceful city, not... not like this. Martin must be losing it."

"What are you looking for?" I asked, confused. Before Linda could answer, Logan entered the office, his voice cutting through the tension.

"Why would Martin be freaking out, Linda?"

Linda jumped and took a couple of steps away from the computer, crossing her arms defensively.

"Well, isn't it obvious?" she said, her voice wavering. "A council member is dead, and it happened on city property. Martin is our manager. He cares about his job. He must be under a lot of stress."

Logan nodded slowly, though his sharp gaze suggested he didn't buy her explanation. I didn't either. But now wasn't the time to press her.

Beside him, Bruno stood alert. The sight of him usually comforted me, but today even he seemed all business.

"What happened here?" Logan asked, carefully stepping around the mess as he approached Linda's desk. Bruno sniffed at the scattered papers, his movements deliberate and precise.

"I don't know," Linda said, her tone shifting from panic to irritation. "I called the police hours ago, but you're the first to show up."

Logan's eyes flicked to the computer. "Was this also sabotage, or—?"

"I don't know!" Linda cut him off, crossing her arms again. "I haven't checked yet. I'm not an IT technician."

Logan put his hands on his hips, fixing her with a hard stare. "But this is your computer. If someone tampered with it, you're the first person who'd notice. If there's something I need to know, I'd rather you tell me now than at the station."

Linda's eyes filled with tears, and she looked away. "I... I don't know. I haven't had a chance to check yet."

"Logan," I said softly, stepping between them and touching Linda's arm. "We were just about to check when you arrived. Linda's already shaken. Can you be, I don't know, a little kinder?"

Logan sighed, his shoulders relaxing slightly. He turned to me, his expression softer. "Fine. But I need both of you to leave everything as it is. My team will examine everything."

"But the meeting—" Linda protested.

"I'm not sure there'll even be a meeting tomorrow," Logan interrupted.

I stepped in before Linda could argue.

"Linda, it's okay. Take the day off. Celebrate your husband's birthday. I'll handle things here."

Linda gave me a grateful smile, grabbed her purse, and left without another word.

"Why did you do that?" Logan asked, his annoyance now directed at me.

"She's clearly upset," I replied.

"And she might know something," he countered, gesturing to the chaotic office. He wasn't wrong, and guilt pricked at me.

"I'm sorry," I murmured. "Let me help."

Logan groaned, running a hand through his hair. "You're unbelievable."

Heat rushed to my cheeks. Was that a compliment or an insult? Before I could figure it out, two more officers entered the office, and Logan turned his attention to them.

I retreated to my desk, determined to find everything I could on the proposal Logan had asked about. He'd need it, and I needed to feel useful.

Chapter 6

The more I read about this proposal, the more uneasy I felt.

At Monday night's meeting, Norman had brushed it off, making it sound like a minor issue that just needed a bit more research to make everyone happy. The Mayor had barely said anything, offering a few words of support for Norman. But Council member Hudson? He'd erupted, accusing everyone of ignoring the city's best interests.

At the time, I hadn't thought much of it. Hudson seemed to oppose anything the Mayor supported. But now? Now I wasn't so sure. This proposal had more conflict swirling around it than anything I'd worked on in my entire career.

"That bad, huh?" Logan's voice cut through my thoughts.

I jumped so hard my chair squeaked, and I barely stopped myself from letting out a small scream.

"Can you be louder?" I shot back, pressing a hand to my chest to calm my racing heart.

Logan chuckled, palms up in surrender. "Maggie, you knew I was on the other side of this paper-thin drywall." He pointed toward the half-wall with its wide window that gave my office a little privacy.

I rolled my eyes and gestured for him to come in. "Where's Bruno?"

"Oh, I see how it is," Logan smirked, raising an eyebrow. "Bruno gets all the attention."

I shrugged, fighting a smile. "He's just too cute to forget."

Logan stepped inside, taking the seat across from me. "He's grabbing lunch and taking a stroll. You know, he gets all the perks."

I chuckled, but my good humor faded as he picked up a folder from my desk and started skimming through it. The reason for his visit hit me like a weight, and my earlier unease returned.

"I don't know if it's bad," I admitted, "but it's definitely not good."

Logan glanced up from the papers. "What do you mean?"

"This proposal... It's been a huge deal in the city, Logan. They've received complaints from both sides, but the biggest issue is how it's been handled. So far, I can't figure out who initiated it, much less how it even got approved for a grant application. There's no paper trail. No one's taking responsibility."

Logan leaned forward, his brow furrowing as he looked at the papers scattered across my desk.

"Some of my friends were upset about losing a rink," he said, "but I don't remember anyone mentioning a grant."

"Exactly!" I said, leaning toward him. "The city is supposed to inform residents about changes—whether it's something small, like licensing a new store, or something big, like converting an ice rink into a pool. That costs serious money. And there's nothing—no records of community engagement, no outreach. I even tried contacting the former director, but he's been ignoring me."

Logan rubbed his face and frowned. "When did you try to reach Troy?"

I resisted the urge to roll my eyes. Of course, Logan knew the guy on a first-name basis. They probably played baseball—or hockey—together. "I emailed him last week after I took the job and followed up on Monday. Left a voicemail Tuesday. Nothing."

"Why did you want to talk to him?"

"I needed to know what to expect," I explained, returning my attention to the documents.

Logan's mouth twitched. "You wanted him to spill all the city's dirty secrets, huh?"

"No!" I said, shaking my head. "This is my first time leading an entire department, and it's... overwhelming. I used to manage the natural resources program—just me and two staff members." I sighed, slumping back in my chair. "This is bigger than anything I've handled before."

Logan rested his elbows on the desk and met my eyes. "Maggie, you have nothing to worry about. Apple Creek is lucky to have you back."

I let out a humorless laugh. "Sure. And my first week on the job? A murder took place at one of our sites, possibly explained by missing documents. All in a day's work, right?"

"This isn't your fault," Logan said firmly,

his tone pulling my gaze to his. "Unless you killed Hudson, which I'm pretty sure you didn't, none of this is on you."

As he approached the desk, my four-legged furry friend ran into the office, interrupting him. Bruno leapt up, placing his massive paws on Logan's chest and nearly toppling him.

"Bruno! Down!" Logan barked, trying to push the dog off, but I couldn't help laughing.

"Oh, you think this is funny?" Logan shot me a look as Bruno wagged his tail, oblivious to the chaos he'd caused.

I crouched down and called him in the sweetest tone I could manage. "Bruno! Come on, boy."

Bruno focused on me right away; after I petted him, I got up. I didn't need to say a word; he just sat perfectly content next to me.

Logan gave Bruno and me a suspicious look. He mumbled something about understanding the guy's choices, but I pretended not to hear. That was the last thing I needed again.

"Anyway," Logan said, "what I was going to say—leave these papers here and go home, Maggie. Spend the rest of the day with Darcy."

Logan smacked his leg and Bruno approached him.

I opened my mouth to protest, but Logan held up a hand to stop me.

"If I need anything, I'll call. Otherwise, we'll pick this up on Monday. This is my investigation, not yours," he said with a smile. "Go home, Maggie."

I followed Logan's advice and drove home, expecting some peace and quiet. But when I stepped inside, I was greeted by chaos instead.

"There you are!" my mom exclaimed, rushing toward me. It wasn't unusual for her to hug me, but I can see fear in her eyes. My heart raced as panic flooded me, my mind jumping immediately to my daughter.

"What happened to Darcy?" I asked, looking around the room.

"Darcy? She's fine," my mom replied, pointing toward the window.

I pushed her to the side to get a better look at the backyard. Darcy was playing by the swing set, giggling as she twisted it around. Relief washed over me, loosening the tight band in my chest as I exhaled slowly.

"It's you I'm worried about."

"Worried about me?" I turned back to my mom, but my sister was already barreling toward me from the kitchen.

"Are you okay?" Sandie grabbed my shoulders, her wide eyes searching mine. "Please tell me you didn't get arrested."

"Arrested?" I frowned, looking between the two of them. "Why on earth would I—"

"Linda stopped by," my mom interjected, sinking into a chair and clutching her chest like a character in an old drama. "She said the police were at your office and wanted to question you!"

Sandie huffed, crossing her arms. "Honestly, I can't believe no one killed Hudson sooner."

"I wasn't sure if Sandie's bitterness was justified, but the fire in her voice made it hard to argue."

"Sandie!" My mom turned on her with a look that, even as an adult, made me flinch. "We do not speak ill of the dead."

Sandie rolled her eyes. "Being dead doesn't make him a saint, Mom. Hudson was the reason so many things went downhill in this city."

"That's not entirely true," my mom countered. "The whole council—"

"He's the one who pushed to cut funding for anything he didn't think was *'appropriate for his residents,'* Sandie snapped, mimicking air quotes.

My mom sighed and softened her tone. "Honey, those decisions weren't personal. I know they affected you and Paul, but it wasn't an attack on your family."

"I wouldn't be so sure," Sandie muttered.

I stepped closer, but Sandie launched into an explanation before I could ask.

"Hudson was arrogant and narcissistic, and he only got elected because he had connections."

"You're saying people bribed others to support him?" I asked.

"There's no proof, but right after he got elected, the Development Department started fast-tracking projects left and right." She gave me a pointed look. "And Paul's company wasn't on Hudson's good list, so guess who didn't get any contracts?"

My mom sighed again, brushing off the

tension. "Politics is always messy, Sandie. It's not worth getting worked up over."

Sandie folded her arms, her voice sharp. "Easy for you to say, Mom. You didn't lose your job because of one of those politicians."

That caught my attention. "Paul lost his company?"

Pain flickered in Sandie's eyes, and she nodded, her voice shaky. "It happened last week. Paul didn't want to tell me. I found out last night when we were talking about a trip to the city. We can't afford anything extra right now." She placed a hand on her rounded belly, and a tear slipped down her cheek.

"Sandie," I whispered, stepping forward to hug her. My mom joined in, the three of us wrapped in a family embrace.

After a moment, I pulled back, brushing Sandie's hair from her face. "Everything will be okay. You're not alone in this."

She smiled faintly and wiped her tears. "Thanks, Maggie. I just... I'm glad you didn't get in trouble like Linda said you might."

I frowned. "What exactly did Linda say?"

My mom busied herself filling the kettle, the clatter of porcelain on the counter jarring. "Linda's a sweetheart, but she has a knack for making mountains out of molehills. She said the police were questioning you—Logan, specifically."

"She said Logan demanded answers from you," Sandie added, shaking her head. "I can't believe he's a detective now. Unbelievable."

"That's a bit of an exaggeration," I said quickly.

"So what actually happened?" my mom pressed, her eyes sharp.

I hesitated, guilt gnawing at me. "There was a break-in at the Parks Department. Linda wasn't involved, but she showed up while I was sorting through the mess. Logan asked me to stay and help him locate some documents."

Sandie's expression hardened. "Maggie, you're not a detective. The last time you played investigator, it didn't end well. Don't you remember?"

I rolled my eyes. "Things didn't end badly, Sandie. I'm not looking to get involved. It just... happened."

Before Sandie could argue, the back door burst open, and Darcy and Toby came racing in, laughter trailing behind them. Darcy flung herself into my arms, and Paul followed behind, looking worn down.

I hadn't seen him in a while, and his appearance startled me. His eyes were ringed with dark circles, and his hands were raw and red, like he'd been working too hard for too long—a strange sight for a Sunday evening.

"Hey, my two handsome men!" Sandie greeted them with a very different tone, scooping Toby into a hug. She leaned in to kiss Paul, who flinched slightly at her touch. "How was the game?"

The shift in focus was a welcome reprieve, giving me a moment to gather my thoughts. I hated the thought of murder, but I also couldn't stand the chance of Hudson ruining my brother-in-law's business. I had to solve this.

Chapter 7

I was helping my mom with the dinner dishes when the doorbell rang. She smiled at me and kept scrubbing a pan, clearly expecting me to answer it. I sighed silently, drying my hands on a towel as I headed to the door.

The second I opened it, a furry blur launched itself at me. Two massive paws slammed into my chest, forcing me to step back as a warm, wet tongue dragged across my cheek.

"Bruno!" Logan's voice rang out behind the dog, sharp and commanding, but the dog ignored him entirely.

"Bruno, no!" I said, trying not to laugh, and, of course, failing miserably.

"Down, Bruno!" Logan barked again. This

time, Bruno dropped to a sit, though his wildly wagging tail betrayed his excitement.

Logan's expression was a mix of irritation and embarrassment as he wrestled with Bruno's leash. "Sorry about that," he muttered, not meeting my eyes as he untangled the mess of straps.

"It's fine," I said, crouching to scratch Bruno behind the ears. "Though I have a feeling he's not the most disciplined K-9 at the station?"

At my side, Bruno whined softly, his ears drooping in what looked like doggy shame. I smiled, ruffling his fur. "He might not be the best-behaved, but he's definitely the cutest."

Logan finally freed the leash and looked up. For a brief second, his mouth twitched into the faintest smile before his usual serious expression returned. "He was our chief's partner until recently," he said quietly, his voice heavy with something unspoken.

I opened my mouth to ask, but his sharp gaze stopped me cold.

"I thought we agreed to talk Monday at the office," I said, trying to lighten the moment.

Logan sighed, shoving his hands into his pockets. "I should've known you'd be here."

I raised an eyebrow, forcing a grin. "Sorry to disappoint you?"

For a moment, he just stared at me, his expression unreadable. A shiver ran down my spine.

"Is Paul here?" he finally asked.

My heart skipped a beat. That's when I noticed the patrol car parked at the curb, with two uniformed officers standing beside it. My pulse quickened, and the air suddenly felt colder.

"I—uh..." My thoughts spiraled. Paul had just lost his job after his company went under. According to my mom and Sandie, he'd always been outspoken, especially about Hudson's council proposal—the one that threatened the local hockey programs he loved. A knot tightened in my chest. "He's in the living room. Let me—"

"I just need to talk to him, Maggie," Logan said, his tone softening as though he could see my panic. "It's just a few questions."

I nodded stiffly and stepped back inside.

My mom's eyes were on me the second I walked into the kitchen. "What's wrong, Maggie?"

Her voice snapped me out of my thoughts. "Where's Paul?" I asked, already heading toward the living room.

Paul was on the couch, engrossed in a hockey game on TV. "Paul," I started, but the words caught in my throat. *The police are looking for you* felt too blunt, and *Logan wants to talk to you* wasn't much better. I took a deep breath. "There's someone at the door for you."

His relaxed expression vanished instantly, replaced by wariness. Without a word, he got up and walked to the door. My mom and I followed, unspoken worry hanging heavy in the air.

Logan greeted him with a curt nod. "Evening, Paul."

"For you to show up here, at my mother-in-law's house, at this hour?" Paul's voice was sharp. "It's about Mrs. Taylor, isn't it?"

Logan's expression didn't waver, though a flicker of something—regret?—crossed his face. "I'd like to ask you a few questions."

Paul's jaw tightened. "I'm not answering anything. Not to you, and not to them." He nodded toward the officers by the patrol car, crossing his arms.

"Paul," Logan said, his tone steady, "I'm trying to handle this quietly—"

"Quietly?" Paul's voice rose. "You call showing up with a patrol car and uniforms quiet? Unless you're here to arrest me, I've got nothing to say."

Logan's patience snapped. "Suit yourself," he said curtly. In one swift motion, he grabbed Paul's arm, twisted it behind his back, and pressed him against the porch railing.

The metallic click of handcuffs echoed through the night as Logan recited the Miranda rights.

My mom gasped, clutching my arm, but I couldn't move. My pulse thundered in my ears as I watched the officers step forward to help Logan escort Paul to the patrol car.

Paul struggled, shouting curses and threats, but it didn't faze them. When they shoved him into the backseat, I noticed Sandie standing on the sidewalk. She was holding Toby in one hand and Darcy in the other, both kids visibly upset.

I'd forgotten Sandie had taken the kids to her house to grab toys. Seeing her there, with tears streaming down her face as she watched her husband get hauled away, shattered something inside me. Before I could run down to her, Logan whistled, and Bruno immediately trotted to his side. He opened the car door for him and glanced at me. Guilt etched lines into his face, but I couldn't bring myself to meet his eyes.

Instead, I turned away and scooped Darcy into my arms. She was sobbing, clutching at my shirt. Toby grabbed my hand, his small fingers trembling.

Behind me, Sandie was screaming at Logan—all rage and heartbreak—but her voice barely registered. I focused on the children, whispering reassurances I didn't believe as the patrol car drove away.

If we'd arrived at the police station at the same time as Logan—or even before him—it wouldn't have surprised me.

The moment Sandie snapped out of her initial shock, she bolted for her car. I didn't need my mom to tell me to go with her. I gave Darcy a quick kiss on her forehead, forced a smile, and murmured that everything would be fine. Then I gently placed her into my mom's arms and sprinted after my sister, barely managing to jump into the passenger seat as she backed out of the driveway.

Though I was glad to be with her, I regretted letting her drive almost immediately. Sandie gripped the steering wheel like it was the only thing tethering her to sanity, but her erratic driving and muttered frustrations weren't helping either of us. The moment she parked at the station, I snatched the keys from the ignition.

She shot me a glare that could've melted steel, but there was no time for an argument. Sandie threw the car door open and stormed inside.

"Where is Paul?" she shouted the second we entered, her voice ringing out in the tiled lobby. She marched straight to the front desk. "Where is my husband? You have no right to take him!"

A young, wide-eyed officer behind the desk froze like a deer in headlights, clearly unsure how to handle her. Sandie leaned forward, her hands slapping the counter. "I'm talking to you! Where is he?"

Before my sister could escalate further, I stepped in, doing my best to stay calm.

"Excuse my sister," I said with what I hoped was a soothing tone, ignoring the furious look Sandie shot me. "She's just really worried about her husband. Paul Sullivan—he was arrested outside my mom's house not too long ago."

The officer, whose name tag read *Tricia Green*, started to respond, but a familiar voice cut through the tension.

"They're fine, Tricia," Logan said as he walked out from the back of the station, his tone steady and authoritative. "I'll talk to them in my office."

Officer Green gave him a look I couldn't quite decipher—equal parts understanding and frustration, maybe? When she turned back to us, her expression was more neutral, but I caught the faintest hint of irritation as she buzzed open the glass door beside her.

Sandie didn't wait for any kind of invitation. She stormed past Tricia, her heels clicking sharply against the floor. I followed close behind, shooting the officer an apologetic glance as I passed. By the time I caught up, Sandie was already halfway to where Logan stood waiting for us, his face unreadable.

I'd be lying if I said walking so deep into the police station didn't unnerve me. It didn't matter that I'd done nothing wrong, or that I was following someone I'd considered a friend—or at least a friendly acquaintance—until tonight. My nerves were on edge, my palms sweaty, and my voice unreliable.

Sandie, on the other hand, had no trouble expressing her anger. Each of her stomping steps seemed to echo through the station.

"You had no right to take him!" she shouted at Logan as he opened the door to a small office and stood by the frame. "He's innocent, and you know it!"

Logan sighed, gesturing for us to step inside, but Sandie crossed her arms and didn't budge.

"Sandie," he said, running a hand through his hair. "I had an order to arrest him. We have evidence that—"

"Evidence!" she practically spat the word. "What evidence? That he lost his job because of that stupid council member? He wasn't the only one, you know. Did you arrest everyone else? Paul's entire company?"

I touched Sandie's arm, trying to calm her, but when she brushed me off, I grabbed her and forced her to step into the office. She turned on me, her face flushed with anger, but I didn't give her the chance to speak.

"You're making this worse," I said in a low,

firm voice. "Logan doesn't owe us an explanation. The least we can do is hear what he has to say."

Sandie frowned at me, her lips curling in disbelief. "Logan? We're on a first-name basis now?"

"Yes, Sandie," I replied as I gently guided her into a chair. "Since we were in elementary school."

She rolled her eyes and turned slightly away, her anger simmering. I knew she was hurting, but sometimes she acted worse than Darcy on a bad day.

Logan moved behind his desk but didn't sit, crossing his arms as he addressed us. His glare shut Sandie up before she could say anything.

"Paul is in big trouble. I won't sugarcoat it," he said. "I can't share details, but there's a reason we arrested him."

He sighed and let his arms fall to his sides, his gaze shifting to me. His expression softened, and I saw concern in his eyes instead of frustration.

"Between us... he needs a lawyer. A good one."

Sandie's hand flew to her mouth, and her face crumpled as she dropped her head into her hands. I didn't need to see the tears; I could hear them in her shaky breaths. I felt useless and furious, but there was no time to dwell on it. Thinking quickly, I asked, "Can we—can Sandie—see him?"

Logan shook his head, his lips pressing into a thin line. "They're finishing the booking process. We need to question him, but he won't talk without a lawyer, so we're waiting for that."

"What kind of questions?" I pressed, already suspecting the answer. When Logan raised an eyebrow, tilting his head slightly, it only confirmed what I'd feared. The questions had been forming in my head since the moment he showed up at my mom's door.

"Paul isn't cooperating," Logan continued. "It's going to be a long night."

Sandie's pale face lifted, her voice trembling as she asked, "He has to stay here all night?"

Before Logan could respond, a knock sounded at the door. Officer Green peeked in, and Logan excused himself, leaving us alone in the office.

Sandie grabbed my hand, her grip so tight I had to bite back a wince. "What am I going to do?" she whispered, her voice breaking. "You know Paul. He's so stubborn, and he's going to be furious. He'll never talk to them."

I couldn't deny it looked bad that Paul refused to cooperate. But I knew him—he was incapable of hurting anyone. He was a big, fluffy bear of a man. Still, if my suspicions were right, and this all had to do with the skates, I needed to find out for sure.

"Sandie," I whispered, crouching in front of her. That's when I noticed the wagging tail and floppy ears of Bruno. He was lying on a plaid dog bed in the corner, a small orange ball resting by his nose. He wasn't sleeping, just watching me intently.

"Bruno," I called softly. His ears perked, and his tail thumped against the floor, shaking his whole body with excitement. "Come."

"What are you—" Sandie started, but her words were cut off as Bruno bounded over. I barely managed to stand before his front paws landed on my chest, forcing me back a step.

"Down!" I whispered firmly, and to my surprise, he obeyed, sitting at my feet with his full attention on me. I scratched his head and grabbed his collar.

Sandie's wide-eyed stare moved between me and Bruno. "What are you doing?"

"I need to get to the ME's office," I said, my

voice low, "but I need an excuse—and a cover here."

Her head shook so fast I thought she might topple out of the chair. "Are you insane? You can't just—"

"Do you want to help Paul or not?" I cut her off, holding her gaze.

That stopped her. She swallowed hard, her lips pressing together, but she nodded.

I turned back to Bruno. "You want to go for a walk?"

His tail wagged furiously, as if he understood every word.

Chapter 8

Although I used to visit the police station to see Chief Ben, my mom's ex, I wasn't sure where to go this time. Somehow, I suspected the morgue would be in the basement, or at least tucked away in a far corner of the building. I felt guilty using Bruno as my excuse to wander. He was such a sweetheart, and I could only hope he wouldn't get in trouble because of me. Judging by the way he sniffed every corner, he didn't seem to share my concerns.

The signs led us down two levels and through a maze of cubicles and offices. I called for Bruno every so often, pretending to chase after him, though it was hardly necessary—every time I said his name, he stopped and waited. Thankfully, no one seemed to notice us.

Upstairs, I just hoped Sandie was selling her act. Most people would be too worried about a pregnant woman in distress to question much. Hopefully, she'd convinced Logan that I'd gone to the car to grab her medication.

The morgue, of course, was at the end of a long, cold hallway. The fluorescent lights above flickered ominously, and for a moment, I felt like I'd stumbled into a horror movie. I chuckled softly as Bruno trotted ahead, sniffing the door. A cheerful dog like him didn't belong in a horror movie.

"Margaret Willow?"

The deep voice behind me made me jump. I whirled around to see a man crouching down to greet Bruno, who had abandoned me without hesitation. Traitor.

"Arthur?" I said, recognizing him instantly despite the years.

His smile spread wide as he stood up. "You remember me! Arthur Cooper."

Relief washed over me, and before I could stop myself, I hugged him. He stiffened in surprise but quickly relaxed.

"Uh, hey," he said with a laugh. "Good to see you, too."

I stepped back, embarrassed but grateful. "Sorry, Arthur. It's been a long night."

"I can imagine." He gestured to the door behind me. "Let me guess—you're looking for me?"

"You're the ME?" I asked, surprised.

He nodded and opened the door. "That's me."

I didn't wait for an invitation. Stepping into his office, I tried to suppress a shiver. It wasn't just the cold—it was the sight of the morgue through the window on the far wall. Rows of metal doors lined the tiled room, and a single steel table sat in the center. At least it was empty.

Bruno, unbothered by the eerie setting, hopped up on his hind legs to nudge a jar off a filing cabinet with his nose.

"Coming, coming," Arthur muttered, rushing to save the jar before it hit the floor. Bruno barked, circling excitedly as Arthur opened the lid.

"This guy," Arthur said with a laugh, handing Bruno a treat. "He comes by all the time. No patience, though."

I smiled faintly but didn't comment. I wasn't here to critique his dog-training skills—I needed his help.

Arthur's tone shifted abruptly. "Look, Maggie, I know why you're here. First of all, you shouldn't be, and second, I can't help you."

"I don't know what you're talking about," I said innocently. "Bruno ran off from Logan's office. I was just trying to catch him."

Bruno, lying on the floor with his treat, looked up at me with wide, trusting eyes. I bit my lip to stifle my guilt.

Arthur sighed. "If Bruno brought you here, you're fine. Forest won't blame you. That dog knows his way around the station better than most officers. But Maggie, I can't tell you anything about Paul."

I considered playing dumb, but decided against it. Instead, I glanced around the office. Arthur's desk was spotless except for a child's drawing—a pair of stick figures in what looked like a park.

"Your kid draw that?" I asked, steering the conversation toward family.

"No," he chuckled. "My niece. She's quite the artist."

I smiled. "Darcy draws pictures like that all the time. Usually of her family. Is that you two?"

Arthur nodded, his expression softening.

I sniffed and cleared my throat for effect. "Sorry, it's just... Sandie's a wreck. Toby doesn't understand what's happening, and with the baby coming..." I trailed off, glancing at the door. Even Bruno seemed to sense my distress, standing at my side with his ears perked. "Who's going to be there for her if Paul isn't?"

Arthur handed me a tissue. "Maggie, I get it. I really do. But I can't—"

"Even bad news is better than not knowing," I said, meeting his eyes. "Please, Arthur."

He hesitated, then sighed. "You didn't hear this from me. Understood?"

I mimed zipping my lips, and Arthur dug through a stack of folders on his desk.

"Forest found Paul's hockey bag," he said finally.

I frowned. "Okay, but how—"

"One skate was missing," Arthur interrupted. "His work ID was in the bag, so there's no question it's his. And Maggie... the police already found the alleged murder weapon. A hockey skate."

My stomach dropped. "That doesn't necessarily mean—"

"It matches Paul's skate. Same red laces. I'm waiting on DNA results, but..." He trailed off, shaking his head. "They found it in a dumpster behind the rink."

"There has to be some explanation," I insisted.

Arthur lowered his voice. "A blow to the head killed Hudson. I have no doubts it was from a skate, but... I found traces of some kind of white powder on his skin. I don't know what it is yet."

A low, familiar voice cut in from the doorway. "I suppose there has to be an explanation for you being down here, Maggie."

My heart lurched as I turned to see Logan leaning against the frame. His eyes flicked between me and Arthur, his expression unreadable but tense.

Arthur straightened immediately, closing the folder and shoving it into the stack. "Forest! What a surprise seeing you. Down here, no less."

"I know, Cooper," Logan said coolly. "You hate visitors—unless they have four legs. But Maggie's special, isn't she?" His tone was light, but there was an edge to it.

Arthur flushed, shoving his hands into his coat pockets. I wanted to defend him, but Logan stepped closer, his hand gently but firmly gripping my elbow.

"Your sister's still waiting for her medication, Margaret."

The use of my full name sent a flush of guilt through me. Arthur looked at me, his expression torn between concern and apology. I mouthed a quick "thank you" and "sorry" as Logan steered me out of the office.

As the door shut behind us, I glanced at Logan. His grip on my elbow loosened, but his sharp eyes never left my face. Did he overhear everything? If he had, he wasn't letting on—yet. My stomach churned. This wasn't part of the plan.

Sandie didn't say a word while I drove us back home, but the moment my mom opened the door and confirmed—again—that Toby and Darcy were sound asleep, she broke down.

"This is a nightmare!" she wailed, trying to keep her voice low, though I lingered near the stairs in case the little ones stirred.

My mom guided her to the couch, her tone calm and practiced. "Maggie, make some tea, please."

I sighed internally. There was something

about tea that Mom swore could mend any crisis. Failed a test? Tea. Got dumped? Tea. Husband accused of murder? Better make it a double brew. I filled the kettle and set it on the stove, rifling through the assortment of herbs in Mom's cabinet.

From the kitchen, I could hear Sandie's muffled sobs. Her words were a garbled mess, but I had a good idea of what she was saying. Thank God she hadn't been with me when Arthur spilled about the skates and hockey bag. That news would have crushed her.

Still, I couldn't shake my own doubts. Paul was hiding something. I knew he didn't kill anyone, but if he was innocent, why not talk to Logan? Why let suspicion fester?

"You have to help me!" Sandie's desperate voice pulled me from my thoughts as I carried the tea to the living room.

"Of course, Sandie," I said, handing a cup to Mom, who promptly pressed it into my sister's trembling hands.

Sandie's tear-streaked face broke my heart. No matter what it had been—a mean girl, a broken toy, or now something far worse—I'd always been there for her. And she'd been there for me.

But her next words made my stomach

knot. "I know you've solved a crime before," she said, her voice rising slightly.

"Sandie—"

"With him!" she interrupted me, her eyes narrowing. "You and the traitor figured it out years ago. Don't pretend you don't remember."

I froze, my pulse quickening. Mom shifted uncomfortably, taking the other cup from my hand. I avoided her gaze, but Sandie wasn't wrong. Years ago, I'd helped Logan solve a case.

"That was different," I said carefully, setting my tea on the coffee table and taking a seat across from her. The space between us suddenly felt necessary.

"Different how?" Sandie demanded, crossing her arms. "Someone died then, too!"

Mom hushed her sharply, then walked to the stairs to check on the kids. As soon as she was out of earshot, I leaned closer and lowered my voice. "It was different. Logan and I just stumbled onto that crime."

Sandie raised a skeptical brow. "You mean you found the dead body?"

I winced. "Yes, and I needed to find the truth before we both got blamed for it. Do you also remember Mom's reaction?"

"Of course. She freaked out when she found out," she said.

I couldn't help frowning. If she knew how much it had worried Mom, why was she bringing it up now?

"Sandie, I didn't have a choice back then. The situation was... complicated," I said, glancing at the stairs. Mom was making her way back to us. "Besides, I promised—"

"Promised who? Mom or Ben? Because Ben is gone and—" Sandie's voice cracked, and she turned to plead her case again. "Maggie, this is Paul! He's being accused of something he would never do, and no one believes me. You have to help!"

Sandie finished her plea just as Mom walked into the living room. Her sharp gaze turned to me. "What does she mean? You are not acting as a detective again, Maggie."

Sandie ducked her head, realizing her mistake, but it was too late.

I sighed, deciding to say everything I'd learned that night. "I went to talk to the medical examiner."

"Margaret Willow!" Mom snapped, standing with her hands on her hips. "What were you thinking?"

"I was trying to—"

"Do you want to help your sister?" she interrupted, her tone icy. "Then we'll find Paul

Flippers, Blades and Murder

the best lawyer we can. But that's it. A man has been murdered. This is dangerous, and I don't need my daughters getting themselves involved."

Sandie's tears started up again. "Mom, no one believed me," she said, her voice so broken that Mom softened immediately, sinking back onto the couch and wrapping her in a hug. "All those officers think Paul did it. Maggie could help me—help my family."

Mom brushed Sandie's hair back and sighed. "Maggie isn't a detective, sweetheart. She got lucky once."

Sandie turned to me, her red, swollen eyes full of desperation. "Paul didn't do it, Maggie. You know that."

I swallowed hard. "I know," I said softly.

"Then help me," she pressed.

My chest tightened. "Sandie, I'll check the R-Parks' files to see if there's any evidence that can prove Paul's innocence. But that's as far as I'll go. Finding the real killer—that's the police's job." I cleared my throat, trying to sound casual. "Did anything Paul said about yesterday strike you as odd?"

Mom gave me a long, measured look, her lips pursed in thought. "What are you thinking?"

"I think," I said slowly, "we need to figure out where Paul was yesterday. He must have a reason for staying quiet."

Sandie's brow furrowed. "What do you mean?"

"Do you know where he was?"

Her face crumpled, and tears welled up again. "He told me he was working on a project for his company."

The words hung heavy in the air. I could see the moment realization hit her. Paul had lost his job the week before.

"Sandie," I said gently, "we both know Paul. He's not a bad person. He's a big, goofy dad who loves you and Toby. Don't lose sight of that."

She nodded, sniffling. "But I don't know where he was. He lied to me."

Mom hugged her again, stroking her hair.

"Maybe one of his friends knows," I offered. "Anyone come to mind?"

"Norman," Sandie said after a long pause. "They play hockey together. He'd know."

"Norman Beltran?" I asked, surprised. The image of the awkward guy didn't exactly scream hockey player.

"Yes."

Flippers, Blades and Murder

"Okay," I said with a nod. "I'll talk to him in the morning."

But as I climbed the stairs later that night, my mind wouldn't stop racing. There were too many missing pieces, too many questions. I kept telling myself I was only helping Sandie figure out where Paul had been. The rest? That was Logan's job.

Or at least, it should have been.

Chapter 9

I decided to start extra early on Monday and arrived at the Community Center while only the most dedicated early skaters were practicing. Walking around the open ice rink, I briefly considered stepping into the restricted rink but thought better of it. Instead, I headed to the Zamboni storage room.

I wasn't entirely sure what I was looking for, but the nagging feeling that someone had been skulking around that area the day before had kept me awake half the night. Arthur mentioned that the police found Paul's hockey bag in the dumpster outside the rink, but it didn't sit right with me. If someone had just committed murder using a skate, why toss the whole bag but leave the incriminating skate behind?

Flippers, Blades and Murder

Dim light seeped into the space, while the faint sounds of skaters scraping the ice, upbeat music, and coaches shouting drifted in from the other side of the rink. As I maneuvered through the narrow space between the walls and the Zamboni, I kept my eyes on the wet floor, careful to avoid slipping. The cooler system often left the mats damp and slick. I spotted the opening beneath the floor—a maintenance pit, much like those in car garages, used for accessing the Zamboni's engine.

It wasn't exactly a welcoming place, and I was about to leave when the door to the larger storage area between the rinks creaked open, spilling a stripe of light into the room.

"Sorry," a young man said, startled to see me. "I didn't know anyone was in here. This area is for authorized personnel only."

I turned to him briefly, but my attention snagged on a faint whitish glimmer underneath the Zamboni.

"Of course," I said. "I'm Margaret Willow, the new R-Parks director."

His face flushed as he stuffed his hands into his pockets. "Oh! I'm so sorry, ma'am—uh—sir—boss?"

I chuckled, crouching down toward the

pit. "Margaret is fine. Do you have a flashlight?"

The young man nodded, darting back into the storage area and returning almost immediately.

He crouched beside me, handing me the flashlight. "Did you see something moving? We've had a few complaints about noises in this room, but I haven't seen any mice."

The thought of mice scurrying around my feet made my skin crawl, but I shook it off, pointing the flashlight into the pit.

"I certainly hope there aren't any mice," I said, aiming the beam toward the white spot beneath the Zamboni. "But do you know what that white substance is down there?"

He squinted into the light, frowning. "I'm not sure... I have to resurface the ice in half an hour. After that, I can take a closer look. I didn't notice anything unusual last night when I locked up."

I stood up, brushing off my hands. "We haven't been introduced."

He quickly wiped his hand on his shirt before extending it toward me. "Oh, right. Sorry. I'm Harold Whitestone, the head janitor here."

"Of course," I said with a warm smile,

shaking his hand. "I've heard great things about your work."

His face reddened further, making him look even younger—mid-twenties at most. "I could move the Zamboni now, but the figure skating coaches will—"

"No, no," I interrupted. "The last thing we need is a complaint from the Skating Club. I know how precious ice time is."

Harold looked relieved as we walked together back into the storage area and its adjoining small offices. The space hadn't changed much since my skating days: cleaning supplies, garbage bins, cleaning carts—a large, organized mess.

"Could you take a picture of that spot once you move the Zamboni and send it to me? I might not be able to come back in half an hour. My phone number is listed in the directory."

"Of course," Harold said, straightening with a smile. "I'll also ask Jack if he noticed it this morning while cleaning the ice, though he's not the best with details."

I nodded. "I'd appreciate that, Harold. And if you ever need anything from the department, let me know. I'm here to help."

As I exited the Community Center, the yellow tape blocking access to the other rink caught my eye. A part of me wanted to peek inside, but I kept walking.

I'd already gotten into enough trouble at the police station the night before, and I knew my mom doubted I'd stay uninvolved. Still, that thought nagged at me as I headed to City Hall.

I made my way to the department offices on the third floor and was surprised to find the main door wide open—again. My heartbeat sped up, but I managed to put one foot in front of the other and, from the doorway, called out, "Hello?"

A loud bump came from under Linda's desk, followed by a groan and some shuffling that ended with another thud against the side of the desk.

"Ouch!" a male voice said as a pair of feet emerged from under the desk.

"Sorry," Terry Larson muttered, crawling out. Linda's desk wobbled with his movements, and a little flower in a small vase toppled over. "Oh, no. I hope I didn't break that."

I picked up the vase, confident it was intact

since it was made of plastic, and placed it back where it belonged. Meanwhile, Terry used the rolling chair to push himself up—nearly falling again in the process.

"Are you okay?" I asked, stepping forward to help.

"Oh, yes," he said, brushing himself off and moving cautiously. "Just a little clumsy this morning."

It was hard not to smile at him. His shy smirk and relaxed posture suggested this wasn't his first mishap, and he'd long since made peace with it.

"What brings you here so early?" I asked. "Is there a program I forgot about?"

"Oh, no," he replied, glancing at Linda's desk. "I was just looking for a flash drive."

I followed his gaze to the cluttered area. Though the mess was limited to the desktop and hadn't spilled onto the floor, it was far from organized. Clearly, Linda hadn't returned to the office since the break-in.

"Linda took the day off," I said, watching his expression darken for a split second. "It's her husband's birthday."

Terry nodded a little too quickly, which only heightened my suspicion. "Right, the birthday. Of course. I just..." He let out a forced chuckle. "Totally forgot what day it was. It is Monday, right?"

I nodded, smiling politely. "Can I help you look for the flash—"

"No!" he interrupted, practically jumping to his feet and heading for the door. "That won't be necessary. I don't want to bother you with something so trivial. I'll just ask Linda."

I gave him a look—one Darcy had come to recognize as the "you're not fooling me" look. Terry froze, clearly uneasy under its weight.

"Later, we'll meet to play pickleball, like every Monday," he said. "Of course! Unless there's, uh... an emergency or—"

"No emergency," I said, keeping my voice calm but firm.

He laughed nervously as he backed into the hallway. "Great! See you later!"

The moment he was out of sight, I turned back to Linda's desk.

The pile of papers was daunting, and I had no idea what I was looking for, but two things nagged at me. First, Linda had been here on a Sunday, outside regular hours—just as Terry was now. Second, if Terry and Linda played pickleball every Monday, it was strange that Terry claimed to have forgotten her husband's birthday. Something didn't add up.

Then, a wild thought struck me. The day before, when Linda seemed upset and eager to leave, she had still stopped by her desk. Could she have taken the flash drive with her—or tried to?

I suddenly wanted to check her computer. But before I could act on the impulse, Tara appeared in the doorway.

"Thank goodness you're here!" she exclaimed, dropping her bag onto Linda's desk. "The mayor is about to shut down all our programs. We can't let that happen!"

I shook my head, trying to process her words, when Martin walked in, looking equally frazzled.

"Oh, good, you're both here," he said. "I left you a voicemail, Maggie. The mayor called an emergency meeting in the Chambers. We need to leave now."

Tara grabbed her bag and fell into step behind him.

I rummaged through my purse, until I found my phone. Sure enough, I had a missed call from Martin. I must not have heard it while I was at the rink.

I was grateful I'd made it to the office in time, though irritated that the mayor could summon us with less than an hour's notice. Something about it felt off.

As I was about to leave, a folder on Linda's desk caught my eye. Bold handwriting in permanent marker labeled it: **POOL GRANT**.

I hesitated, then pulled it from the pile. The first page was an illustrated document titled *Grant Request to Convert Ice Rink to Lap Pool*.

An unsettling feeling churned in my stomach. Yesterday morning, I thoroughly examined the proposal, but I didn't find a grant request or any reason to proceed in that direction. I didn't have time to read it in full, but I scanned the bottom of the page. The approval signature belonged to Council Member Hudson, dated two months ago.

"Are you ready?" Martin called from the door. "We can't be late."

"Yes, sorry," I said, sliding the folder into my purse. Something was very wrong with this project.

Chapter 10

By the time we walked into the conference room, the large table was nearly full. Two other council members were already there, but the Mayor had yet to arrive. I followed Martin and took a seat between him and Tara. Almost immediately, Tara began pulling documents from her tote bag, which only made me feel more unprepared and anxious.

Scanning the table, I recognized only Norman. He was fixated on his phone, typing furiously, his expression as troubled as it had been the day before. Judging by the speed of his typing, he seemed desperate to get his message across to whoever was on the other end.

"This is outrageous!" A woman's voice

echoed from the hallway, and everyone in the room looked up.

"If you're going to do nothing, what good are you to this city? My people have been waiting far too long for answers, and this crime is just proof of how poorly we've been treated!"

Her voice grew louder as she approached the room, but most people quickly returned to their own business.

"It's nothing," Tara whispered, pulling my attention away. "That's Mrs. Taylor, the chair of the Charter Commission. She sounds like this every day."

The large woman I'd seen yelling at Norman yesterday appeared in the doorway. This morning, she was dressed in a bright yellow sweatsuit, her makeup so heavy it made me wonder how early she'd woken up to apply it.

To my surprise, she was shouting at the Mayor, who was at least a head shorter than her and looked positively diminutive in comparison. His expression was one of barely restrained frustration, which only seemed to fuel her anger.

"This is going to be a long meeting," Martin muttered beside me. "It was going to be anyway, but if she comes in..."

Tara nodded without looking up from her papers. "I hope he shuts her down. Though, if he hasn't managed that by now, I don't know why today would be any different."

"Well," Martin whispered conspiratorially, "she's made it very clear that it was 'her support' that got him elected."

I couldn't help myself. "That sounds wrong on so many levels." Politics obstructing the City's well-being was something I couldn't stand.

Martin turned to me, serious but not annoyed, so I continued.

"Even if she endorsed him, that doesn't mean she put him in office. Unless she bought the election, which I hope isn't the case."

Martin nodded, lowering his voice further. "Besides her involvement with the Charter Commission, she runs a nonprofit that helps kids access extracurricular activities. According to her, their support and votes secured his victory."

"That's still a stretch," I replied. "Unless her organization is the size of half the city."

Martin chuckled, but the conversation ended as the Mayor stormed into the room, followed closely by Mrs. Taylor, who planted herself in the chair directly behind me. Since she wasn't part of the city's staff or Council, she had no seat at the table, but it was clear she intended to make her presence felt.

The Mayor didn't waste any time. With a sharp bang of his gavel, the room fell silent.

"Thank you all for coming," he began, scanning the room. "As you're well aware, a tragic event occurred yesterday at one of our facilities—"

"Bah!" Mrs. Taylor's derisive exclamation cut through his words.

"Do you disagree, Tonia?" the Mayor snapped, his tone barely masking his irritation.

Behind me, I heard her chair scrape against the floor as she stood. "A murder is not an accident, Henry. At least have the decency to call it what it is."

Across the table, the Mayor's face darkened. I suddenly understood why he'd been so prickly about being addressed by his title in our previous meeting—clearly, he was used to people undermining his authority.

"The death of Council Member Hudson is indeed tragic," the Mayor said, his voice strained. "That is why I've called this meeting—to discuss how the city will respond. If you'll allow us to work, you might get some answers."

Mrs. Taylor muttered something under her

breath, but she sat back down with an audible thump.

The Mayor straightened and addressed the room again. "As I was saying, this is a deeply concerning situation. I've received numerous calls and emails from residents expressing their fear and disgust. In light of this, I'm shutting down all recreational events, lessons, and programs until the police resolve this matter."

The room erupted in murmurs, council members whispering to one another but not directly addressing the Mayor. Behind me, Mrs. Taylor launched into another tirade, her words dripping with disdain.

"With all due respect, Mayor Dosal, I don't think this is the best course of action," I said before I could stop myself. My pulse pounded in my ears as the room fell silent and the Mayor fixed me with an icy glare.

"Mrs. Willow," he began, and I bristled at the incorrect title. "You just arrived here. You can't possibly know what's best for our citizens. The complaints I've received make it clear what the people want, and running empty programs benefits no one."

"Not one complaint has reached the Recreation and Parks Department," I said, subtly correcting him. "This morning, the ice rink was packed with skaters, and the seniors were happily taking their yoga classes. Tonight, the pickleball courts are booked."

The Mayor opened his mouth, but I pressed on.

"Shutting down our programs will only increase panic. The murder of Council Member Hudson is a tragedy, yes, but it's not a reason to upend our entire department's work."

Council Member Laurens spoke up. "Miss Willow is right. Residents rely on these programs. Some have already paid for them, and others depend on them to keep their kids safe while they work."

"And what about the calls and emails I received?" the Mayor countered, his tone sharp.

Council Member Roberts leaned forward, his voice steady and authoritative. "I received only a handful of inquiries. And I find it peculiar that you're the only one claiming an overwhelming number of complaints."

The tension in the room was suffocating. Everyone seemed frozen in place, waiting to see who would crack first.

"Are you accusing me of lying?" the Mayor demanded.

Roberts smirked. "Is that what you did?"

Martin cleared his throat, cutting through the charged silence. "What happened to Council Member Hudson has shaken all of us. Miss Willow took the initiative to assess the Community Center this morning, and it's clear that closing our programs will do more harm than good. We should focus on communicating what we know and keeping residents informed."

Council Members Laurens and Roberts nodded in agreement, but the Mayor remained rigid, his face a mask of fury. Before he could respond, Mrs. Taylor leapt to her feet.

"You have to close the rinks!" she shouted, advancing toward the Mayor. "What is this, a reward for murder? Those hockey players should be banned from this city!"

Her hateful tone struck a nerve. I stood, my voice steady but firm. "You have no right to make such a ridiculous demand. You don't work for this city, and your personal vendettas have no place in this meeting."

Mrs. Taylor gaped at me, momentarily stunned into silence.

"All programs will continue as planned," I said, turning to the Mayor. "The Recreation and Parks Department is committed to serving this community, and we will not let fear dictate our actions."

Without waiting for a response, I gathered my papers and walked out of the room.

Although I made it to the elevator, the moment I pressed the button and waited for it to arrive, my knees started to shake, and my hands wouldn't stop trembling. I wasn't sure what had come over me—probably the stress of knowing Paul was being accused of murder or the fact that I was, once again, somehow involved in a murder. Whatever the cause, at least I had said my piece. Or so I thought.

"Who do you think you are?"

I recognized Mrs. Taylor's voice instantly and saw her stomping toward me. At first, I didn't think she was addressing me—not until her yelling continued.

"You have no idea who I am, and you think you can just come in here and yell at me?"

The elevator doors slid open. Tempted as I was to step inside, I didn't. Instead, I stayed put, realizing something had to be wrong with me. Most people, when faced with someone twice their size barreling toward them, would take a step back. Me? I took a step forward, forcing her to stop in her tracks.

"You have no authority in my department," I said firmly.

She let out a loud, mocking laugh and looked down at me with undisguised contempt. "Authority? I own your department. And it's only a matter of time before I destroy those rinks. I was going to settle for just one to make room for a lap pool, but now? Now I'm closing both and building an Olympic pool."

My mind raced, piecing together her outfit, the rushed proposal, and her smug attitude. Whatever she thought she owned or controlled, I was certain it couldn't be legal. And her smug smile? That made it personal.

"Over my dead body," I said before I could stop myself.

Only after the words left my mouth did I realize the weight of what I'd said—especially to someone who might actually be a killer. Her face shifted, shock momentarily replacing her confident smirk.

The elevator bell dinged behind me, but I couldn't take my eyes off Mrs. Taylor. She raised her index finger and pointed it at me, her towering frame emphasizing the threat in her stance. My thoughts split in two: How long would it take for her to actually reach me from that height? And how badly would it hurt if she did?

Before either question was answered, someone stepped between us, gently sliding me back a step.

"What's going on here?"

Logan's voice was calm, but it carried a weight that instantly broke the tension.

"This woman was verbally assaulting me," Mrs. Taylor declared, her voice dripping with indignation.

I frowned, ready to retort, but Logan didn't let me.

He placed his hands on his hips and stared her down. For the first time, Mrs. Taylor seemed to realize that Logan was taller than her —and that the patch on his belt marked him as law enforcement. At my side, I felt a familiar warmth press against my leg, and without looking, I knew Bruno had joined us.

"It's interesting you call it assault," Logan said evenly. "Because from what I saw, it looked more like you were threatening Miss Willow."

Mrs. Taylor straightened, lifting her chin in defiance. "This won't stay like this, officer."

Logan smiled—a cool, unsettling smile that

even made me feel uneasy. "Detective Logan Forest."

"Ah!" Mrs. Taylor exclaimed, her demeanor shifting briefly before her condescension returned. "So it's you I have to thank for arresting that hockey criminal last night. Too bad you've just disappointed me."

Bruno, now sitting squarely on my foot, was the only reason I didn't leap at her and punch her.

"Well," Logan replied, his voice steady, "I'm glad my job doesn't depend on your approval."

Mrs. Taylor huffed, shaking her head as she stepped into the elevator. The doors slid closed behind her, and the moment they did, I groaned, though what I really wanted to do was scream.

"Hey," Logan said, his hands gently gripping my shoulders as he leaned down to look me in the eyes. His concern caught me off guard, and for some reason, it upset me even more. "Are you all right? Did she try to hurt you, or—"

"I'm fine," I cut him off, stepping back to put some distance between us. "What are you doing here?"

He sighed, running a hand through his

hair. "I thought we were going to talk about the proposal."

Before I could respond, Norman's voice rang out from the hallway.

"Margaret!" he shouted, grinning ear to ear as he approached. "That was awesome!"

I frowned, confused, but didn't have to ask.

"We're keeping our programs open! And you've got two new fans—Council Members Laurens and Roberts. I don't think Roberts has ever liked anyone before!"

Only then did Norman seem to notice Logan standing there. He turned his attention to him, scratching Bruno's head in the process. Bruno welcomed the affection and leaned slightly against Norman's leg, asking for more.

"You should've seen her, man," Norman said, practically beaming. "She shut down the Mayor's ridiculous idea *and* Mrs. Taylor—all in the first five minutes of the meeting!"

Chapter 11

Norman eagerly recounted his version of events to Logan, though I didn't fully agree with his retelling. I hadn't yelled at the Mayor or anyone else, and while I disagreed with his decision, I didn't recall challenging his reasoning for shutting down the programs quite as dramatically as Norman claimed.

Still, I didn't interrupt his story because my phone rang, pulling my attention away.

It was Harold. He explained that he hadn't forgotten to send the picture—he'd just struggled to find my phone number. That was on me for relying on the directory. I thanked him for the update and told him not to worry. After hanging up, I gave the photo a closer look.

At first glance, it appeared to be a dimly lit, empty section of a garage or storage room. But as I zoomed in, a few details stood out: buckets against the walls, the last step of what looked like a pit, and water pooling along the edges. Then, my eyes landed on a whitish stain near the pit's edge. It looked as though something had splashed and dried there, leaving behind a conspicuously cleaner patch of concrete compared to the surrounding dirt and oil stains.

"Isn't that right, Maggie?" Norman's voice pulled me out of my thoughts.

I looked up to find both men staring at me, waiting just outside the elevator.

"What was that?" I asked, scrambling for a response. Without waiting for an answer, I stepped out of the elevator and headed down the hallway toward my office.

Norman and Logan followed me into the office, though Norman was clearly more enthusiastic about it.

"I was just explaining to Logan how the Mayor claimed to have received complaints from residents," Norman said, closing the door behind him. "What do you think that's all about?"

I shook my head as I walked to my desk. "Who knows? Maybe it's election season?"

Norman frowned. "He just got elected."

I sighed, lowering myself into my chair. "Like I said, I don't know. And since he's probably going to fire me anyway, I really don't feel like guessing."

Logan, leaning against the doorframe with his arms crossed, straightened at my words. But it was Norman who spoke up with a laugh.

"He can't fire you. That's Martin's job, and Martin won't do it. He was as ecstatic as Roberts during the meeting."

I opened my mouth to argue, but stopped myself. As much as I hated to admit it, I didn't want to lose my job. If Norman was right, I didn't want to jinx it, either.

Norman grinned and bounced on his heels. "Besides, I don't want this workload again, so I'll threaten to quit if I have to."

His comment managed to pull a smile from me. "Thanks, Norman. I hope it doesn't come to that."

"I agree," Logan said, stepping inside the office. "No one should be threatening anyone around here."

His casual tone sent a spark of irritation through me. Before I could stop myself, my voice sharpened. "What do you think you're doing?"

Bruno's ears perked up at the shift in my tone, and Norman instinctively took a step back, closer to the large window that served as one of my office walls.

Logan stopped mid-step, lifting his hands in mock surrender, a small chuckle escaping his lips. "I just told you—I came to talk about the proposal. Or whatever you've figured out about it."

Crossing my arms, I lifted my chin. "I have nothing to say to you."

Norman cleared his throat, clearly ready to excuse himself, but Logan shifted slightly, unintentionally blocking the doorway.

"You have no right to be mad at me," Logan said, his voice quiet but firm. "As I recall, it was you who broke into the station last night."

My blood boiled. "I broke into—you gave me no choice!"

Norman glanced nervously between us, signaling toward the door as if asking for permission to leave. Neither of us budged.

"I gave you no choice?" Logan leaned closer, narrowing his eyes.

"Yes!" I planted my hands on the desk, the sound echoing in the room. Norman flinched, covering his mouth with one hand.

Flippers, Blades and Murder

"Hey, guys—" Norman started, but I cut him off.

"I went to the station hoping you'd calm my sister down. Instead, you got all official and serious, claiming you couldn't say anything to us!"

Logan's eyes widened. "Claiming? Maggie, I can't tell you anything. I'm a detective—"

"Oh, I know that very well," I snapped, leaning over the desk. "It was crystal clear last night when my five-year-old watched you drag her uncle into a police car in handcuffs! And Sandie? Do you have any idea the kind of night she had?"

Logan stepped back, his gaze dropping to the desk.

"Believe me, Maggie, that wasn't the plan."

"Well, as long as it wasn't part of the plan," I said, my voice trembling with anger.

Logan looked up at me. "Paul could've just cooperated. You were there. He could've answered my questions, but no—he let whatever grudge your sister has against me get in the way of a murder investigation." He leaned in again, this time too close for comfort. "Maggie, a man is dead. My job is to figure out who killed him. I don't have time for high school drama."

His words stung, mostly because they

might've been true. Still, I wasn't ready to let him off the hook.

"In that case, let's settle this right now." I turned to Norman, who seemed to shrink into the corner.

"Sandie told me you and Paul are friends. Where was Paul last Saturday?"

Norman's eyes darted between me and Logan. "I think he had to finish a—"

"Don't," I interrupted. "I know he lost his company a week ago, so he wasn't finishing anything. Where did he go?"

Logan crossed his arms, his eyes narrowing at Norman. "Do you know something about this?"

Norman fidgeted, stammering. "I—I really don't know much. He told me to cover for him with Sandie because he missed our tournament, but... I don't know where he went."

Logan's tone sharpened. "What do you mean he missed the tournament? Wasn't he playing hockey this weekend?"

Norman hesitated, his face flushing. "He told me he'd be there, but when I got to the rink in Maple Hollow, he wasn't. Jordan said Paul claimed he forgot his gear at the Community Center. I thought he'd show up later, but he didn't. When I called him on Sunday, he said the tournament was a waste of time and money, but he asked me to say nothing to Sandie."

His words hung heavy in the air. My shoulders sagged, and I rested my head on the desk, overwhelmed by frustration. Bruno nudged my lap, his warm presence a small comfort.

Logan crouched and patted his knees, coaxing Bruno away. "Come on, boy." He glanced at me as Bruno reluctantly trotted over. "Maggie, you need to talk to Sandie. She doesn't need more bad news from me."

With that, Logan left, and neither Norman nor I felt like working the rest of the day.

"Miss Willow," a shy voice called from my office door. I was surprised to see Harold standing there, hovering by the frame.

"Harold," I said with a smile. "What can I do for you?"

Norman stepped closer and extended his hand to Harold. "Hey! Fancy seeing you here. What brings you to this building?"

Harold glanced at me, his gaze dropping to my desk as he mumbled, searching for the right words. Something about his demeanor was off.

"I called him," I said casually, though I didn't feel as composed as I sounded. "I had a few questions after walking past the rink this morning."

Norman's eyes widened in concern. "I can help you!"

"It's all right, Norman. I know you're busy, but thanks for the offer."

Harold lingered by the door until Norman walked out. He cast a nervous glance over his shoulder, toward Norman and the rest of the department bustling outside my office.

"Can I close the door?" he asked, his tone low and alarming enough to send a chill through me.

"Of course," I said, trying to keep my voice steady.

Once the door shut, Harold exhaled deeply and sat in the chair across from me. For a fleeting moment, the thought crossed my mind: could Harold be the killer? But then he spoke.

"I went down to the pit to take the picture you asked for. Everything seemed normal at first—even that weird white stain—until I

Flippers, Blades and Murder

came back up. That's when I noticed something strange about the rubber seal on the back door leading to the loading lot."

He fidgeted with his hands, avoiding my gaze.

"Harold," I said gently, leaning forward. I waited until he met my eyes. "Just tell me."

"It might be nothing, Miss Willow."

I nodded, offering a reassuring smile. "If it's nothing, then there's nothing to worry about. I promise."

He sighed, running a hand through his hair. "You see, it's summer, and we have to work hard to keep the ice frozen. Everyone on my team knows how important it is to keep those doors closed and the seals tight. It saves a ton of energy."

My patience was starting to wear thin, but I knew pressuring him wouldn't help.

"So, I left the pit, ready to give someone an earful for leaving the door like that. But as I got closer, the door just... opened wide. And that's when I saw the buckets."

"Buckets?" I asked, my curiosity piqued.

Harold nodded. "Yeah. In the lot, leaning against the wall on the opposite side—the wall of the other rink. There were bleach buckets."

"Bleach buckets? You mean like gallon bottles?"

"No," Harold said, lowering his voice. "Bleach powder. The kind they use in pools."

Alarms went off in my head, though I didn't yet understand the full gravity of what he was saying.

"Is that powder dangerous?"

Harold tilted his head, considering. "Yes and no. It's a chemical, so it has to be handled carefully. But we don't use it at the Community Center, and we definitely wouldn't leave it outside in the lot. Anyone could grab it."

My mind flashed to the white stain in the pit—the strangely clean spot on the otherwise grimy concrete.

"Did you tell anyone about this?" I asked.

Harold's hands trembled slightly, and worry etched lines across his forehead.

"I told Bert—he's in charge of the facilities—but by the time I found him, the buckets were gone."

"Someone moved them?"

He nodded, glancing nervously toward the office windows. "Bert told me to forget about it. Said I must've seen something else. But I know what I saw."

Flippers, Blades and Murder

I nodded, but before I could respond, Harold continued.

"I didn't show him, but I took a picture." He pulled his phone from his pocket and scrolled through his photos. "I used to help out a few nights a week at the pool—just to make extra money. It didn't take long to walk around the facility and make sure everything was in order." He shook his head. "Right after Mr. Archer, the last R-Parks director, left the department, Mrs. Taylor came to the ice rink looking for me. She made it very clear that I should stay away from the pool or I'd get fired. I didn't want to just send this photo... you'll understand when you see it."

Harold handed me his phone. The image showed three large buckets, clearly labeled **Bleach Powder.** But what stood out was the sticker on the last bucket: **Property of Apple Creek Swimming Club.**

I raised my eyes to meet Harold's.

"You get it now!" he exclaimed.

"The Swimming Club? Yes, but—"

Harold leaned forward, lowering his voice again. "We're not supposed to talk about this, Miss Willow, but that club has been behind every push to shut down the ice rink. Those people are full of lies, and there's no reason any

Montie Red

of their stuff should be here. There are even rumors of them committing fraud."

"I guess it's time I paid them a visit," I said. Before Harold could protest, I added, "Send me the picture. Don't worry—I won't tell anyone where I got it. And thank you, Harold."

Chapter 12

Apple Creek didn't have a large aquatic center, but we did have a small splash pad in one of the parks and a lap pool in the park's community building—one we shared with the middle school. It had been years since I'd visited that part of town, though not for any specific reason. I'd probably just outgrown the splash pad, and I hadn't found the time to take Darcy. I made a mental note to bring her one day. She and Toby would love playing around the sprinklers, and the forecast predicted warmer weather later in the week.

I made my way to the pool building, expecting the familiar sound of children laughing and splashing in the water. Instead, I was greeted by eerie silence. The pool was half-empty, and no one was around.

My suspicions grew as I walked along the edge of the pool toward the locker rooms. The metal bleachers were partially closed, and piles of debris and materials were scattered across the tiled floor.

To my recollection, there had been no mention of the pool being under construction, and there certainly hadn't been a sign outside the building to warn visitors.

"This is private property!" someone shouted behind me.

Startled, I turned to see Mrs. Taylor storming out of an office on the second-floor balcony.

"You!" she barked, hurrying toward me.

I can't lie—this time, I grabbed my phone and held it firmly in my hand, ready to call the police if needed. I also glanced over my shoulder, noting the pool's edge behind me, and stepped a little farther from it.

"Mrs. Taylor," I said as she approached, her pace quick and deliberate. "This is city property. What are you doing here?"

She stopped just short of bumping into me. "You have no business here," she snapped.

"I beg to differ," I replied, crossing my arms and mirroring her snarky tone. "This is part of the Recreation and Parks programs, and I am the director."

She huffed, tossing her hair back. "You're not my director. I am the president of the Swimming Club, and you have no authority here."

I could have argued that the Apple Creek Swimming Club was just a nonprofit organization running one of the programs the city pool offered, and the facility was my concern. We had other programs too—or so I vaguely recalled—but I didn't have all the facts, and I wasn't here to debate that. I decided to let it slide.

"So, as the president of the Apple Creek Swimming Club, I'm sure you're aware of everything happening with this nonprofit, correct?"

Mrs. Taylor straightened her posture, glaring down at me. "That's correct, but I don't have to discuss anything with you. This isn't your concern. The city has no weight in my nonprofit."

"I'm not so sure about that," I said, holding up a finger to stop her from interrupting me. "If you know everything about your so-called nonprofit, explain to me why your bleach powder buckets were outside the ice rink."

I wasn't sure what kind of reaction I expected, but the way her face drained of color and her eyes widened wasn't it. She hesitated, mumbling as she glanced over her shoulder toward the office she'd just come from.

"Is someone up—"

"No one else is here!" she snapped, cutting me off. Her confidence wavered for a moment before she continued with a forced air of authority. "I don't have to answer to you. Do you even have proof of what you're claiming? If that's all, you should leave. This is private property, and—"

I wanted to show her the photo Harold had given me, but something held me back. A nagging sense of self-preservation reminded me that someone had already been murdered. Instead, I shifted tactics.

"This isn't private property, Mrs. Taylor," I said, shaking my head. I took a step back but held my ground. "Like I said, this is city property. If I see another incident like this, I'll remove your club from this pool."

"You can't—"

"Yes, I can," I interrupted, watching her

face change again. This time, while not pale with fear, her features softened with concern.

"And I should," I added, gesturing at the mess around us. "Where is everyone? It's the middle of summer. Kids should be swimming. This pool should be packed. Isn't that the reason you requested an additional facility—the overwhelming demand for swimming lessons?"

Mrs. Taylor took a step forward, her composure returning. She launched into what sounded like a well-rehearsed explanation.

"Kids prefer to be outside in the summer, not stuck indoors. If you really want to help, we'd love an outdoor pool or a full aquatic center. But for now, we'll settle for the new pool at the Community Center. The distance people have to travel to get here is another reason attendance is low. Just because you don't see anyone right now doesn't mean this space isn't being used or paid for."

Her answer only raised more questions in my mind, but before I could respond, a loud crash echoed from the upstairs office.

"For heaven's sake!" Mrs. Taylor exclaimed, spinning on her heel.

She stomped back toward the office. "See yourself out, Miss Willow," she called over her shoulder. "You have no business here. We run all the swimming programs. You should ask your staff; clearly, you're not up to speed on how we do things around here."

Another loud crash followed as more objects fell, the sound echoing through the empty pool area. Something very strange was happening here, and I didn't like it. Even if it seemed unrelated to Hudson's death, my gut told me this wasn't the end of the story.

I returned to my office, trying to shake off the strange encounter at the pool. Everything else seemed perfectly normal, except for Linda's absence. The department was alive with its usual buzz of activity, just as it had been the previous week when I was still learning the ropes of the job.

Tara was waiting for me, looking slightly anxious. I just hoped this wasn't about the Mayor trying to shut down our programs again.

"Margaret," she began as I motioned for her to walk with me. "First, thank you for stepping in at the meeting earlier. I was panicking.

So many parents rely on our programs, and the thought of them being shut down..." She sighed, reaching out to gently touch my arm. "I really appreciate it. Honestly, it should have been Martin defending the programs, not you."

Her voice trailed off, and her eyes drifted downward at the mention of Martin. It was hard not to notice the tension there. My curiosity piqued, but I held back from asking. Though Tara and I got along well, I wouldn't have liked her prying into matters about Andrew or Darcy.

"I was just doing my job, Tara. It's really no big deal."

"Oh, it was!" Her eyes widened. "Especially considering all the trouble poor Troy got into—"

That caught my attention. "What trouble?" I asked, my tone sharpening slightly.

Her cheeks flushed as if she'd said too much. She shook her head and focused on the stack of papers in her hands, clearly hoping I'd drop it. But I wasn't letting this go.

"Tara," I pressed, stopping to face her. "I've been trying to contact Troy for weeks. I know something's off, but I can't fix it if I don't know what's going on."

She shuffled her feet uncomfortably, but after a few seconds, she sighed and relented. "Fine, you're right. But—" She motioned toward my office. "Let's talk in private."

I followed her inside, and she closed the door behind us. I bit back a smile. It was the second time that day someone asked me to talk in private. Something that never happened at my old job and it made me feel oddly fascinated.

"Troy is a good man," Tara began, clutching the papers to her chest. "But he got caught up in... a situation."

She glanced over her shoulder nervously before continuing.

"When Mayor Dosal was first elected, he wasn't exactly popular. Everyone loved our former Mayor, so the comparisons were inevitable. People still talked about how much they missed her. It was a tough act to follow."

I nodded, understanding the challenge. Starting a new role was always hard, and being constantly compared to your predecessor only made it worse. So far, I hadn't faced much of that in my position, but I had a feeling Tara was about to explain why.

"Mayor Dosal wanted to improve his relationship with the community," she continued.

"The problem was, he had no idea how. So he sought Troy's help to brainstorm ways to improve his standing."

She hesitated, biting her lip. "At first, it sounded promising. Improving our programs and adding new facilities seemed like a win. But then... Rufus got involved."

My brow furrowed. "Rufus? What does he have to do with this?"

Tara looked uneasy but pressed on. "Rufus suggested that building an aquatics center would win people over. He even introduced Troy and the Mayor to his mother, Mrs. Taylor. That's when the negotiations started."

"Wait," I said, connecting the dots. "Mrs. Taylor is Rufus's mom?"

She nodded. "The resemblance is uncanny, isn't it?"

A memory of Rufus being unnecessarily harsh to poor Terry flashed through my mind, followed by Mrs. Taylor's icy demeanor earlier. It all started to make sense.

"But isn't that a conflict of interest?" I asked. "Wouldn't any deal benefiting a city employee's family cross a line?"

Tara sighed and sat down. "You'd think so. But the city lawyer explained that as long as Rufus doesn't personally profit and since Mrs.

Taylor's program is technically a nonprofit, it's not a legal issue."

I didn't like the answer, but I couldn't exactly argue with it. After all, Paul was my brother-in-law and worked for the city. I wouldn't want my position to cause problems for his company.

"All right," I said, sitting down across from her. "So what happened?"

"That's where things get messy," Tara admitted. "Councilman Hudson got involved. No surprise there—he always inserted himself into every deal. Troy and Martin signed papers to start a feasibility study for expanding our swimming programs. I know because I read them, and I was there when Martin signed. But now, those papers are gone, Margaret."

Her voice grew quieter as she added, "A week before you started, the local news reported a proposal to dismantle the ice rink and replace it with a pool. Before that morning, none of us had seen that proposal—not even Rufus, or so he claims."

Her eyes were wide with worry. "A demolition company was hired, and I've seen invoices for the initial work. But the ice rink is still intact, and the money... it's missing. All that money from our residents—gone. Hudson was convinced the Mayor took it, but if that's true, then Troy would have to be involved, and I just..." Her voice cracked. "I don't believe Troy would do that. He's a good man."

I kept my voice low. "But what about the pool construction? I didn't see anything—"

"What construction?" Tara interrupted, frowning. "The pool has been running the swimming program all summer. I have the registrations and waiting lists on my desk."

Her expression was earnest, but I needed to be sure. "Have you been there recently?"

"Oh, yes," she said. "I drive by every day and see the kids playing."

"But have you been inside the pool?" I pressed. "Or has anyone else from the department?"

Her expression shifted, resembling anger, but I didn't have the chance to analyze it. I stood. "I need to talk to someone."

Tara jumped to her feet, her panic returning. "You can't tell the police! They won't believe us. We have no proof."

"Tara," I said gently but firmly. "Trust me. I won't break your confidence. But we need to uncover the truth."

I was practically stomping out of the Department when I bumped into Bert—the guy I'd wanted to talk to even before I ran into Tara.

"Bert," I said, turning on my heel. "Can we talk?"

He smiled, as unconcerned as ever, just like the first day I met him.

"Sure, boss."

He started heading toward my office, but I stopped him.

"I need to—just walk with me."

Bert shrugged and gestured for me to lead the way.

Whether it was Tara's unsettling revelations or my tense exchange with Mrs. Taylor, I suddenly felt as if the very walls of City Hall were watching me. Like I was in a horror movie, waiting for something to jump out. Hyper-aware, I kept moving, trying to brush it off. We made it to the elevators without incident.

"I have a question about our facilities," I said as we stepped inside. For the first time since I met him, Bert's expression turned serious—not upset, just focused.

"Of course, boss. How can I help?"

The elevator doors opened, and we stepped into the bustling lobby of City Hall. It was the middle of the day, and people were lined up to pay bills, apply for permits, or file complaints. Probably the worst place for a private conversation, but the noisy crowd provided just enough cover for my question.

"Why would powder bleach be behind the ice rink?" I asked.

Bert frowned, crossing his arms as a couple passed us. "There shouldn't be any of that by the ice rink—or anywhere near the community center. Did someone—"

I motioned for him to follow me to a quieter corner of the lobby, away from the doors and front desk.

"I saw buckets of it outside the closed rink this morning," I said.

Bert's eyes widened, and his mouth dropped open for a second before he leaned closer. "You saw them too?"

I nodded, deciding not to correct him. Explaining Harold's photo felt irrelevant for now.

He exhaled sharply. "I had no idea. That rink's still closed for the investigation, but I needed to grab a cleaning cart from the storage room. We've got a wedding this weekend and need the extra supplies." He shook his head. "Those buckets shouldn't have been there, but then something strange happened."

He glanced around, scanning for eavesdroppers.

"I parked out back with my trailer to load the cart. When I saw the buckets, I was furious. I mean, sure, those snobs from the swimming club think they can do whatever they want, but come on. Anyway, I went inside and had to be careful not to disturb the crime tape or anything." He paused and gave me a serious look. "I had police permission to grab the cart, Margaret. No funny business."

"Well, that's good to know. Thanks."

He ran a hand through his hair, clearly rattled. "Anyway, I was in there for maybe 10, 15 minutes tops. When I came back out, the buckets were gone. Just gone. That's when Harold found me. I had hoped he knew where they went, but he didn't. I take my job seriously—even when I joke around. No vehicles should've been back there, and there's no way someone on foot could've taken them. But I know how that Mrs. Taylor operates, so I told Harold to let it go."

"Any idea who took them?" I asked. When he shook his head, I added, "Why is the swimming club managing the pool's maintenance? Running programs is one thing, but upkeep should be our job."

Bert crossed his arms, nodding. "Exactly. Same deal as the hockey association—they handle lessons and tournaments, but we maintain the ice. They don't touch our facilities, and honestly, that's for the best. Have you seen the concession stand? It's a disaster."

My brow furrowed. "Has it always been like this?"

Bert's smile returned, and somehow it only made me more concerned. "Ever since the Mayor made that deal with the swimming club, they've had control of the pool building. It's basically their problem now. I spoke out against it—loudly—but I lost access to that building. I don't know what's going on in there, but..." He leaned closer, lowering his voice. "Let's just say I'm not surprised Hudson got killed."

I didn't need to prompt him—he continued, his voice dropping further.

"He was all buddy-buddy with Rufus and Mrs. Taylor until two weeks ago, when he pulled all those projects and contracts from the city. He made a lot of enemies that day."

Out of the corner of my eye, I noticed a shadow approaching the window nearby. Before I could process it, I heard a loud crash. Instinctively, I ducked as glass shattered around us.

The lobby erupted into chaos. People screamed, scrambling away from the large windows facing the parking lot. I stood and glanced outside, just in time to see a black SUV peeling out of the lot with a screech of tires. No license plate. No clear make—just shadows disappearing into the distance.

"Everybody stop!" someone shouted.

I turned to see a swarm of police officers rushing into the lobby. It was no surprise, given the station was right next door. Although, the audacity of the attacker—pulling this off right under law enforcement's nose—said a lot.

"Are you okay?" I asked Bert, who was still crouched beside me. His face was pale, his hands trembling.

"What is that?" he whispered, his voice high-pitched, eyes locked on something nearby.

I followed his gaze and spotted a broken brick lying amidst the shattered glass. My heart raced as I approached it, noticing a jagged hole in the window where it had flown through.

As I crouched for a closer look, a heavy weight barreled into me, knocking me onto my backside. Warm fur and an eager tongue smothered me.

"Bruno!" I exclaimed, pushing the big dog's face away as he enthusiastically licked my cheek. "Bruno, stop!"

A sharp whistle cut through the chaos, and Bruno sat back, his entire body wagging with his tail as he stared at me.

"Here," came Logan's voice, just as strong hands grasped my arms and lifted me to my feet.

"You okay?" he asked, turning me slightly to inspect for injuries. His hands lingered briefly before he stepped back, looking self-conscious.

"I'm fine," I said, brushing dog hair off my coat. "Bruno must think I'm his favorite chew toy."

Logan didn't smile. Instead, he ran a hand through his hair and turned to help Bert up. Meanwhile, a nearby officer carefully placed the brick into a plastic evidence bag.

I caught a glimpse of it—white powder dusting the edges and a message scrawled across it: "Stay away."

Chapter 13

"I'm not letting you get involved in this, Maggie," Logan said, his voice sharp as it echoed in his office.

I didn't care. My patience was wearing thin with all the questions and zero answers.

"For all I know, you almost got hurt in the lobby with that—"

"No," I interrupted, crossing my arms and planting myself by his desk. "You don't know what happened there, and I'm not going to dwell on it. Otherwise, I might as well pack up Darcy and move back to the city."

Logan ran a hand through his hair, standing on the opposite side of his desk, frustration etched into his face.

"Let me talk to Paul," I said.

"Paul?" He let out a bitter laugh, though

it lacked any humor. "Your brother-in-law is a piece of—" He grabbed a folder and slid it across the desk toward me. "He's toying with us, Maggie. These are all the lawyers in town, and he's refusing to use any of them or cooperate with us. I'm about ready to send him to State prison and see if he's so bold over there."

My hands trembled, though I hid it well—except from Bruno, who pressed his head against my leg, sensing my unease.

"Let me help," I said firmly.

Logan's features softened slightly, and his tone lowered. "You know I can't do that. He needs to—"

"I'm not asking about the murder," I interrupted.

Logan crossed his arms, skepticism plain on his face. "I don't know if I can trust that."

I lifted my shoulders in mock surrender. "Why not? In case you haven't noticed, I have bigger problems to deal with. He might know what's going on in my department. That's all I need to ask him about."

"Your department?" Logan raised an eyebrow. "Why would Paul know anything about R-Parks?"

I sighed and began pacing, trying to find

the right words. It wasn't a matter of trust—it was a matter of where to start.

"Forget the murder for a second," I said. "There have been too many strange things happening in R-Parks—things tied to the swimming club and that proposal I mentioned to you."

Logan didn't interrupt, his full attention locked on me.

"It might be nothing, but I've heard rumors that..." I hesitated. I hated spreading gossip without proof, but the situation was spiraling, and I needed answers before anyone else got hurt. "I can't confirm this, but apparently, the Mayor, Hudson, and Troy were working on a project to boost the Mayor's image with residents."

Logan nodded slowly. "I've heard of that—it started when the Mayor took office. Over a year ago."

"So there is a deal," I stated, watching as Logan smirked.

"Are you interrogating me now?"

I waved a hand, dismissing his joke. "The deal itself isn't the problem. The problem is how they decided to convert an ice rink into a pool at the Community Center—and why my department lost management of the pool. Now the swimming club is tangled up in all of this."

Logan's smirk faded as he narrowed his eyes in thought. "I get that. So far, there's no paper trail of any study or plan we could find—but also no money changing hands."

I resisted the urge to criticize him for not telling me this sooner. Maybe he intended to, but I hadn't exactly made it easy to talk that morning.

"That's why I need to talk to Paul," I said, leaning over his desk, palms flat on its surface. "His company worked for the City. He has to know something."

Logan shook his head and took a step back—a bad sign. I scrambled for the one card I had left to play.

"The pool is under construction," I said. "And there's no record of any project in that building."

Logan's brow furrowed, his posture straightening. "What are you talking about?"

I stood tall, a flicker of satisfaction blooming at knowing something he didn't.

"I went to the pool this morning. The place is a construction site—no swimming, no lessons, nothing. And it's the middle of summer. Do you know how long the waiting list is for swim lessons in Apple Creek?"

Logan didn't answer, his focus still sharp on me.

"Too long," I continued. "And sure, we have a small outdoor program, but that's it. The building is locked up, and Mrs. Taylor is claiming it's private property."

Logan rubbed his face, turning away briefly before spinning back to me.

"That pool wasn't closed at the start of the summer, Maggie," he said. "I met with Troy there before one of our games."

"I'm telling you, it's strange. And that's why I need to talk to Paul. He might know something. I'm sure of it."

Logan stared at me, his expression unreadable. "What makes you think he knows anything and—" He raised a hand to stop me from answering. "And why would he talk to you?"

I smiled, shrugging lightly. "I'm more charming than you are. And..." I hesitated, searching for a better argument, but finding none. "We're family."

I had to admit, I was partially surprised that Logan had agreed to my request. Sure, he'd given me just ten minutes and was listening from behind the double mirror, but at least I'd have a chance to get a few answers. Or so I hoped.

A police officer brought Paul into the room, his hands cuffed. His angry expression shifted the moment he saw me sitting there alone.

The officer pulled out a chair and gestured for Paul to sit. Paul raised his cuffed hands. "What? You think I'm going to attack my sister-in-law?"

The officer didn't respond and walked out, closing the door behind him.

"Great manners around here," Paul muttered, glancing at the door before turning to me.

He looked terrible. Dark circles ringed his eyes, his face was covered in stubble—something Sandie would never have allowed—and he seemed thinner, paler, though his tan from years of outdoor work was still visible.

"Maggie," he said, his tone softening. "What are you doing here? Are Sandie and Toby okay? Did something happen to them?"

I shook my head, trying to muster a reassuring smile. "They're as fine as they can be, given the circumstances. Toby's scared, and Sandie..." I sighed. "Sandie's a mess, but she's with my mom."

He nodded, avoiding my gaze, his eyes fixed on the door.

"They sent you here to guilt me into talking, didn't they?"

I didn't have time to argue. I'd promised Logan I wouldn't ask about the murder, and I intended to keep my word.

"Someone threw a brick at City Hall," I said, keeping my tone even. "It was likely aimed at me, Paul."

That got his attention. His head snapped toward me, his eyes wide. "What? What happened? Are you okay? Who did it?"

I leaned back in my chair, crossing my arms. "I was hoping you could help me figure that out."

His brow furrowed. "I don't see how I can—"

"What's going on with the pool and the ice rink deal?"

The way his eyes widened and his head shook slowly told me everything I needed to know: he was hiding something.

"I found buckets of bleach powder outside the rink," I continued, "which disappeared minutes later. And the pool is closed, under—"

Paul leaned forward suddenly, his cuffed hands reaching across the table. "You need to stop asking questions, Maggie. This isn't a joke. People—" He cleared his throat and glanced at the double mirror behind me before lowering his voice. "Someone's already been murdered. This is dangerous."

I felt my blood boil. Whether it was the mention of the murder I'd been trying to avoid or the realization that he'd been keeping secrets, I wasn't sure.

"You knew about this and didn't tell me?" I snapped.

"I didn't—I don't—"

I slammed my hands on the table. "Yes, you do! And you knew I was taking a job here and bringing Darcy with me!"

He threw his hands up defensively, leaning back. "Maggie, please. I didn't know anything before—before last week when Hudson—"

Even I could see the fear and guilt in his eyes. A part of me wanted to stop pressing him. He was family, and I felt bad for him. But if he was scared, that meant Darcy and I might be in danger, too.

"Hudson did what, Paul?" I demanded, leaning closer. "And don't you dare stop talking. If anything happens to my daughter or me, it'll be on you."

I thought I heard movement behind the double mirror, but before I could turn, Paul started talking.

"I have nothing to do with this murder," he said, his voice low.

I narrowed my eyes but stayed silent, afraid he might clam up.

"Since I opened my company, I've worked with the city here in Apple Creek. I had a decent relationship with the former mayor, so I expected the same from this guy." He shook his head. "Before Troy left, he and Martin sat me down and told me the Mayor was favoring another company for the big projects. They promised me I'd still get the smaller ones."

I knew just enough about city planning to realize that all projects were supposed to go through a public bidding process. Apple Creek was small, but surely it had more than two construction companies.

"It isn't illegal, Maggie," Paul added quickly, rubbing his face as best he could with his cuffed hands. "Most contractors want the big jobs, not fixing banquet kitchens or whatever."

"I didn't say anything," I replied, though apparently my raised eyebrow betrayed me as I learned when Paul smirked.

"Sandie raises her eyebrow like that when she doesn't agree with me."

"Don't change the subject."

He chuckled but continued. "Everything seemed fine until last week. I'd just sent my crew home after finishing a flooring job when Hudson showed up."

Paul leaned forward again, his voice dropping. "It was a long conversation, but he basically told me I needed to sign some invoices for a work on the pool. I told him I hadn't done the job and wouldn't sign anything."

His jaw tightened, and his knuckles whitened. "He laughed at me. Said the Mayor sold the pool to that woman—what's her name? The one with the wild, colorful sweatpants?"

"Mrs. Taylor?"

He nodded. "Yeah, her. Runs the swimming club."

Paul's fingers fidgeted nervously. "Hudson threatened me, Maggie. Said if I didn't sign the invoices, my company was finished. I still sign nothing and went to the Mayor, but he told me to shut up about Hudson and that woman. Next thing I know, I'm getting an email saying my construction license was being revoked and my company was under inspection from the city."

Anger flared in his eyes as he hit the table. "These people are crooked, Maggie. All of them. I don't trust anyone."

Understanding dawned on me. "That's why you haven't hired a lawyer."

"Exactly!" he whispered. "What would you do? A council member pressures you to sign fake expenses, the Mayor tells you to stay quiet, and suddenly you're accused of murder? How can I trust anyone?"

I glanced at the double mirror, then reached across the table to grab Paul's hand.

"You can trust Logan."

Paul started shaking his head, but I stopped him. "I trust him, Paul. Despite all the evidence, he's still looking into what really happened."

"Maggie," Paul said, exasperated. "He's the one who arrested me!"

"I know, because you wouldn't talk to him. Where were you on Saturday?"

Before Paul could answer, the door opened. Logan walked in, his expression calm but firm.

"Maggie," he said. "We had a deal. You can't ask—"

Paul cut him off. "You want answers? Fine. I'll talk. But she stays."

Paul had a solid alibi. Once he decided to talk, it became clear he wasn't lying. In fact, his life was probably safer at the station than at home —with Sandie.

"Well, it all checks out," Logan said, walking toward me. "It might take a bit to get the paperwork done, but he should be home in time for dinner."

I nodded, still trying to process everything Paul had told me.

"You think Sandie's gonna kick him out?" Logan asked.

The question made me smile, though I couldn't help but feel for Paul. "You know Sandie. Plus, Paul swore to her he'd given up gambling before they got married."

Logan flipped through a stack of papers in his hand and started toward his office. I didn't need to follow, but my feet moved on their own. Bruno's wagging tail greeted me enthusiastically as I entered. I couldn't resist his invitation, crouching down to give him a scratch behind the ears.

"I always thought Sandie's rule was a bit extreme," I said, breaking the silence.

Logan looked up at me, smirking. "Margaret Willow, are you saying you support gambling?"

I chuckled, shrugging. "If you're as good as Paul used to be, maybe."

"How good are we talking?"

I tilted my head, considering. "Well, he was so good, he used to claim his losses on his taxes as deductions."

Logan raised an eyebrow. "Wow. A professional?"

"Sort of." I scratched Bruno's head.

Logan sighed. "He should've told me everything, Maggie."

I stayed quiet, letting the silence speak for me as I focused on Bruno. Finally, I broke it. "Sorry about this morning," I said softly.

Logan's brows shot up in surprise. "Sorry about what?"

"We were supposed to talk about the proposal, but I was mad at you, and... well, it all worked out, right?"

Logan ran a hand through his hair, staying silent a beat too long. My stomach churned, wondering if I'd actually upset him.

"You don't need to wait for Paul," he finally said, changing the subject. "I can give him a ride home or have someone else do it. I don't want Sandie's opinion of me making his life harder."

He was joking, but he wasn't completely wrong. Poor Paul had a long night ahead. My sister wasn't one to forgive easily, especially when promises were broken or she felt betrayed.

"I'm not really waiting for Paul," I admitted, the realization dawning on me as I spoke.

Logan narrowed his eyes, crossing his arms. "Then what are you still doing here?"

"I want you to see the pool," I said, standing up. "You need to see what's happening there for yourself."

Logan didn't move. "I know," he said firmly, "but you're not going, Maggie. I don't know what's going on yet, and I won't let you put yourself in danger."

I crossed my arms, mirroring his stance, and stayed silent.

"You're not planning to go back there, are you?" he asked, though he didn't wait for an answer. Instead, he groaned, running a hand through his hair before heading to the door.

"Let's go, then," he said, his tone exasperated. "Come on, Bruno."

Chapter 14

We arrived at the pool just before sunset. The absence of people near the splash pad made the place feel deserted and somewhat menacing. I couldn't believe no one had raised concerns about it before, but I figured that had to do with Mrs. Taylor's reputation and her insistence that she owned the place.

"I'll give you this," Logan said as he stepped out of the car. "This looks very suspicious."

As I climbed out, Bruno leaped through the open window, landing beside me. To my surprise, Logan handed me Bruno's leash. I gladly took it, wrapping the rope twice around my hand to shorten the distance.

"I'll be damned," Logan muttered, staring at Bruno. "You little traitor."

I looked between Logan and Bruno, unsure of what he meant.

"You've got your theories, I've got mine," Logan said, a smirk tugging at his lips. "This furry partner of mine has been pulling and fighting me every step of the way since I got assigned to him. But the second he saw you this morning..." He shook his head, walking toward the building's entrance. "He listens to you. He's glued to your side whenever you're around."

Unconsciously, I bent down to give Bruno a well-deserved rub behind the ears. "Well, we are old pals, remember? We met years ago when he was just a puppy at Ben's house."

Logan threw his hands in the air and huffed. "Great! How will this help me with my new partner?"

Without waiting for an answer, he opened the door, motioning for me and Bruno to follow.

The hallway inside was as dark as night. The only glimmer of light came from beyond the double doors at the far end. Logan didn't draw his gun, but his hand hovered near it.

When Logan pushed the double doors open, he went in first. The sharp, familiar smell of chlorine hit me, and my eyes were drawn to the rippling reflections of a few lights on the water. The stands were fully set up, ready for a crowd, and the only sign of construction was a blue tarp piled with debris, a couple of hammers, and some buckets.

I walked further in, shaking my head as I glanced toward the office balcony above the entrance. The pristine scene before me was nothing like the mess I'd found earlier that morning.

"Maggie, wait," Logan said, stopping me in my tracks. His tone made me turn. To my surprise, he had his gun out, held low but ready, his eyes fixed on the office.

Before I could ask why, a growl from Bruno and the sound of rapid footsteps drew my attention. A noise came from the balcony, followed by a scream from the second-floor office.

Logan bolted up the nearest set of smaller stairs, skipping two steps at a time. He was nearly at the top when the office door flew open, and a man stumbled out, looking terrified.

"Help!" the man shouted, his gaze locked on the office behind him. "She needs an ambulance! Help!"

"Don't move!" Logan ordered, but the man

startled, tripping by the edge of the stands. Luckily, he landed flat on the balcony's floor instead of tumbling down the steps. That's when I recognized him.

"Bert!" I let go of Bruno's leash and rushed up the steps.

Bruno sprinted toward the back doors leading to the locker rooms, barking and growling as he jumped up against the doors, trying to force them open.

"Who's inside, Bert?" Logan demanded, his gun still aimed toward the office. He barely glanced at me.

I stopped beside Bert, who was trembling, his face pale. He pointed shakily at the open office door. "I didn't do it. She was like that when I got here."

I leaned forward and saw Mrs. Taylor lying unconscious on the floor.

Logan shot a quick look toward Bruno and shouted, "Stop!"

Bruno immediately stood still, his gaze glued to the double doors. Even from afar, I could hear him growling.

Logan crouched beside her, holstering his gun and pulling out his phone. I moved to join him, ready to help. My years of CPR training for my previous job might be useful.

Flippers, Blades and Murder

"I need an ambulance and backup," Logan said into the phone as I reached the doorway. "She's breathing but unconscious."

The office was small—just a desk and a three-drawer filing cabinet. But something about it felt... off. It looked too clean, almost staged. And there was no chair or obstacle that could have caused Mrs. Taylor to hit her head.

"How's Bert?" Logan asked, snapping my focus back to him.

I turned to check. Bert was sitting with his head in his hands, still shaking. "Probably in shock, but..." My eyes drifted back to the room, scanning for clues. No papers on the desk, no safety vests, no signs of wet floor or no running by the pool—nothing. Then I noticed Mrs. Taylor's hands. Both were dusted with a whitish powder, as if she'd been handling flour.

"Logan, don't touch her," I said, kneeling down for a closer look. He moved me back slightly.

"What, Maggie?"

I pointed at Mrs. Taylor's hands, then the faint traces of powder along her neck and hairline. "Arthur mentioned a white powder. What if she's been—"

"We don't know anything yet," Logan interrupted, standing and gently gripping my shoulders to guide me back. "She's breathing. We'll wait for the paramedics. Stay with Bert."

His voice was calm, but the tension in his jaw betrayed his worry. I stepped back, sitting down beside Bert. The sound of approaching sirens broke the silence, and that's when I realized Bruno was missing.

I stood up, scanning the area. "Bruno?" I said, careful not to draw Logan's attention. I didn't want to get Bruno in trouble, and it had been me who lost his leash. "Come on, Bruno."

Bert glanced up at me, confused, but I pressed a finger to my lips, signaling for him to stay quiet as I crept toward the far end of the pool. My heart pounded as I neared the tarp-covered debris. Relief washed over me when Bruno popped out from behind the pile.

"There you are," I whispered, crouching to pet him. That's when I noticed the small pouch in his mouth.

"Drop it," I commanded gently. Since Bruno was ignoring me, I took matters into my own hands and pulled the bag. Then he finally sat down and dropped it by my feet.

It was an old coin purse, the kind people used before credit cards became abundant. Its seams were worn, and I struggled to unzip it. Inside was a small black flash drive.

Flippers, Blades and Murder

I glanced back toward Logan, my pulse quickening as the scene behind me grew louder with paramedics shouting instructions. Sliding the flash drive back into the bag, I tucked it into my pocket.

Bruno growled at the back doors again. My hand trembled as I touched the handle, and the door flew open. Bruno tried to dart outside, but I managed to grab his leash, stopping him. This time, fear gripped me—not just for myself, but for Bruno.

"Let's go, Bruno," I whispered softly, turning us both back toward the others. "We better wait for Logan." My heart was pounding as I thought about the significance of what I had discovered.

If it weren't for the fact that I was sitting on the back of an ambulance, waiting to talk to the police, the sunset might have been beautiful. The sky blazed in shades of orange and pink, but I barely noticed. It had been less than half an hour since we found Mrs. Taylor, though time seemed to stretch endlessly. More than anything, I needed to talk to Logan.

Bert sat nearby, wrapped in a thick blanket as paramedics fussed over him. He wasn't hurt —just in shock. Logan had decided it was better to question him here instead of hauling him to the station, which made sense. But Bert's dazed state didn't inspire much confidence that his answers would clear anything up.

Mrs. Taylor, on the other hand, had been rushed to the hospital. Her condition had worsened rapidly since we found her. I'd tried calling her son, Rufus, but he didn't answer, so I left a voicemail. I disliked the man—and wasn't exactly a fan of his mother either—but no one deserved harm like this.

"Maggie," Logan called, striding toward me with Bruno trotting at his side. As soon as Bruno spotted me, his ears perked up, and he bolted forward, dragging Logan behind him like an anchor.

"Hey, boy," I said, crouching to ruffle his ears.

Logan frowned, but a flicker of a smile crossed his face. "Traitor," he muttered, scratching Bruno's head. Then his expression sobered. "Listen, I'm telling you this because I know you, and I don't want you getting into trouble."

I straightened and narrowed my eyes. "What did you find?"

He sighed. "Nothing."

"Nothing?"

He nodded. "No signs of anyone else being here with Mrs. Taylor. No evidence of what happened to her. Just... nothing."

"What about the construction?" My frustration bubbled over as I gestured toward the building. "Logan, you have to believe me. This morning, it was a mess—piles of materials everywhere, and the pool was half-empty."

Logan rubbed his temple, but before he could answer, Bert spoke up.

"She's right," Bert said, his voice shaky as he climbed out of the ambulance. "I was here yesterday, and Mrs. Taylor kicked me out, but it looked like a demolition site."

Logan's expression darkened, though his tone stayed measured. "I'm not sure about a demolition, but when I said we found nothing, I meant nothing. No paperwork, no swimming equipment, no lifeguard gear—nothing to suggest this building was even operational."

"What about behind the pool?" I asked, my voice rising slightly. "Outside the double doors? Bruno seemed pretty determined to get there."

Logan exhaled, planting his hands on his hips. "There were some tire marks on the gravel, but nothing else. We'll have to check the security footage, though I'm not optimistic. The camera back there... well, let's just say it's probably older than us."

Bert straightened, his blanket slipping slightly. "But you believe us, right? About the construction materials and how everything suddenly looked cleaned up?"

Logan nodded, and Bert sagged with relief —until Logan added, "Have you seen Norman?"

"Norman?" Bert's voice shot up an octave. "What does he have to do with this? I haven't seen him. No, no Norman."

I clenched my fists to keep from snapping at Bert. If he was trying to cover for someone, he wasn't doing a great job.

Logan raised his hands, palms out. "Relax. I just need to talk to him. He's the Operations Maintenance director, and up until last week, he was in charge of this building. If you see him, let him know I'm looking for him."

Bert fidgeted, shoving his hands into his pockets. "Can I go now? I'm not feeling great, and I just... I need to go home."

"Sure," Logan said, his voice even. "But before you do—what were you doing here?"

Bert hesitated, then gave a small nod, avoiding Logan's eyes. "I wanted to confront her. Not physically," he added quickly. "I just... I wanted to know why she's so set on destroying Apple Creek's R-Parks. But when I got here, everything was locked. I went straight to her office, and that's when I noticed the pool was full and the place looked... clean. I didn't knock—I just barged in. That's when I found her and ran out to get you."

"So you arrived just minutes before we did?" Logan asked.

Bert nodded vigorously. "Yes! I came straight from work. You can ask Tara—I was with her until six, then drove here."

Logan didn't look entirely convinced, but he nodded. "All right, Bert. Do you need someone to drive you home?"

"No, I'll manage," Bert said, hesitating over the blanket. "I'll wash this and bring it to the hospital later."

Logan and I both watched as Bert trudged to his car, his steps unsteady. When he finally pulled out of the lot, Logan turned to me, his tone softening.

"So, what do you think?" he asked, then

smirked. "And are you planning to steal some evidence?"

I flushed, covering my face with my hands. "I'm so sorry. I completely forgot."

Logan chuckled, taking the pouch I handed him. His fingers brushed mine, sending an unexpected flutter through my chest. I quickly focused on Bruno, scratching behind his ears to ground myself.

"Bruno found it," I said, my voice steadier. "It was buried under the tarp-covered debris, I think."

Logan stood, offering me his hand. "Come on. I'll take you back to the station."

I hesitated, confused, and he laughed lightly.

"You rode with me, remember? Your car's still there."

"Oh, right," I said, embarrassed. I rose to my feet, walking beside him and Bruno. "For a second, I thought you were going to arrest me."

Logan stopped, his tone serious. "Maggie, I hope I never have to arrest you. But to avoid that..." He lifted the pouch. "If you have time, maybe you'd like to check out what's on this drive with me?"

Flippers, Blades and Murder

Chapter 15

Back in Logan's office, I stood behind him, watching as he plugged in the flash drive.

"Can I ask you something?" I said, breaking the silence while the computer worked.

"You can ask. Whether I can answer is another story."

I narrowed my eyes at him but stayed on topic—I didn't need any distracting arguments.

"Why did you ask Bert about Norman?"

Logan paused, his fingers hovering over the keyboard. He turned his chair to face me, his eyebrows furrowed, his mouth a straight line. He rubbed his chin, visibly working to control his tone.

"I found something."

A chill ran through me, and I stiffened, but I didn't say a word. He grabbed my hand, his gaze steady.

"Before you jump to conclusions," he began, "I don't think it's a coincidence, but I have to follow the facts. Norman's hockey bag—and one missing skate—were under Mrs. Taylor's desk."

The air in the room seemed to shift, turning cold. I crossed my arms over my chest, bracing myself.

"What do you think it means? You don't think Norman had anything to do with Mrs. Taylor, do you? Why would he leave his bag—wait, do you think *she* stole the bag... and one skate?" I asked, lowering my voice as I tried to stop my mind from jumping to conclusions.

Bruno, sprawled on his bed, perked up his head, tilting it slightly as though listening.

"That's exactly what I'm trying to figure out," Logan said, his voice calm but firm. "Let's wait to hear from the hospital before making any assumptions. But I'll need to ask Norman where he was." His tone sharpened. "Maggie, do *not* ask him anything. I'll handle it tonight and let you know what I find. Deal?"

I nodded, but before I could press him further, his computer emitted a series of beeps that drew both our attention. I leaned closer to the screen as the drive loaded. A long list of files appeared, most labeled with dates. Among them was one folder that stood out—**R-P**.

Logan clicked on it, and inside were more files, each with a string of numbers that didn't make immediate sense. After quickly glancing through a few documents that appeared to be meeting minutes or invoices, he discovered something interesting. It was an email from Troy Asher, the former R-Parks director, dated a year ago. Logan and I both leaned in as we read:

Mayor Henry Dosal,

When we agreed to begin exploring projects to improve our city, I believed the plan was to engage with residents and determine what they actually wanted. As I've stated in my previous twenty emails and countless meetings, I do not see the need to expand our aquatics program—let alone move it to a different location, especially the Community Center.

The ice sheets are as much a concern for the Apple Creek Swimming Club as they are for our skating programs and partner associations and clubs—figure skating, hockey, recreational skating—all of which have equal standing in the city. Moreover, there is no indication that these programs are financially unsustainable.

If you proceed with this plan, it will be imperative to involve the residents, whose taxes fund all of these programs. Skipping the necessary steps for a proposal of this magnitude by using the remainder of our past referendum funds is not only irresponsible—it's illegal.

By the time you read this, please be aware that I've already informed the ice users' associations of your intentions.

Sincerely,
Troy Asher
Director, R-Parks

Logan sat back, rubbing the back of his neck. "Have you heard back from Troy yet?"

I shook my head.

He stood abruptly, grabbing his jacket. Bruno jumped up and followed him. "I need to talk to him."

"Maggie," he said, pausing at the door, "please go home. I'll let you know what I find."

"Are you done eating?" my mom asked, pointing at my half-eaten plate.

For a moment, I stared at my food, but I just wasn't hungry. Troy's email kept bouncing around in my head, and Logan's sudden decision to go look for him only made things worse. On top of that, I couldn't shake the feeling that something was profoundly wrong in the R-Parks Department. Now, it seemed like it was my responsibility to figure it out.

"Yes," I finally said, getting up and heading toward the kitchen to help my mom. She stopped me halfway there.

"You look like you need a break, and I know a little one who would love to get ice cream this evening."

I turned just in time to see Darcy's eyes light up.

"I don't know if that's a good idea," I said with an exaggeratedly sad tone. "We probably need to go to Sandie's and check on Paul. He might need rescuing."

Darcy clasped her hands dramatically and pretended to fall to her knees. "Mommy, please! We need ice cream to survive!"

My mom laughed while I shook my head. Darcy could be a bit dramatic when she wanted to be, but she probably got that from me. I turned to my mom. "You also need ice cream to survive?"

My mom shook her head. "Not this time. I'm planning to watch Toby. I'm just putting these dishes away, then I'm heading over to spend the night with your sister."

"Is everything okay over there?"

My mom shrugged as she tossed her apron onto the kitchen counter. "Your sister asked me to stay with Toby. I know she's happy Paul is back, but..." My mom sighed. "She's as stubborn as ever."

"Would it help if you reminded her that, according to the casino, Paul's a winner?"

My mom lightly swatted my arm, frowning at me. "You stay out of it—just like I'm planning to. I'm just going over to check on my grandson."

"All right, then." I turned to Darcy. "Go grab your shoes."

She giggled and ran toward the door to get ready.

"We could meet you there. Toby might need some ice cream, too."

"Oh, boy!" My mom placed a hand over

her heart in mock exasperation. "Now you're trying to get me in trouble with Sandie?"

"What? She doesn't allow ice cream?" I teased, not waiting for an answer. Instead, I walked toward the door where Darcy was waiting. "Remember this, Darcy: you have the coolest mom in the family."

Darcy nodded seriously and threw her arms around me in a hug. "I already know that."

And with that, the night started to feel a little brighter.

"Have fun, you two," my mom said as we headed out. "And don't forget your keys, Maggie. I'm locking up."

A cool shiver ran down my spine. She was probably right to lock up, but it wasn't something she usually did—especially since my sister lived just a few houses down the street.

The moment I opened the door to the ice cream shop, the sweet, creamy aroma transported me back to so many memories of my time in Apple Creek. But it was the familiar voice of Agnes O'Leary, the shop's owner, that truly made me smile.

"Maggie Willow! Your mother told me you were back in town."

Agnes came out from behind the line of freezers and hugged me. It wasn't unusual—she'd been one of my mom's best friends since childhood, and I'd always thought of her as my adoptive aunt.

"You look amazing, Agnes."

She blushed and waved her hand dismissively before bending down to greet Darcy.

"You must be Lucretia's granddaughter! She's always bragging about how smart you are. What grade are you in now? Seventh?"

Darcy chuckled, shaking her head. "No, I'm starting kindergarten!"

Agnes stood back up, placing her hands on her hips with exaggerated surprise. "Oh my goodness! A preschool graduate? That calls for a celebration. What's your favorite ice cream?"

Darcy darted toward the freezer, standing on her tiptoes to see the array of colorful flavors.

"This might take a while," I said to Agnes with a smile.

"That's fine. I'm in no rush. You can take a seat on the patio," she said, pointing toward the back door. From where I stood, I could see patio lights strung up, along with part of a table.

"That's new," I said, stepping closer to get a better look.

"My son, Larry, built it a couple of years ago. Now we can host summer night parties."

The patio was surprisingly busy for a weekday evening. The tables were decorated with small vases of wildflowers and tea lights, complementing the warm glow of the surrounding gazebo. As I turned back toward Darcy, I caught sight of Linda walking toward one of the tables. Sitting with her were her husband, Terry, Tara, and Norman.

"Mommy," Darcy called, snapping my attention back to her. "Can I get two scoops? Please?"

I turned to find Agnes looking at me with a knowing smile.

"Sure, Darcy, but get them in a bowl," I said.

Darcy squealed with excitement and went back to inspecting the freezers.

"Everything all right, Maggie?" Agnes asked gently, her perceptiveness catching me off guard. I hadn't realized how poorly I was hiding my mix of frustration and concern.

"Could you keep an eye on Darcy for a minute?"

Agnes smiled warmly, a reminder of why I thought of her as family. "Say no more. I'll give Darcy a tour of the kitchen."

A big part of me wanted to join that tour—Agnes's kitchen was where the magic happened, and she always shared little surprises. But I had questions that needed answers, especially after the day I'd had and the direction things seemed to be heading.

I didn't hesitate as I walked toward the table, even when Logan's warning of not talking to Norman came to mind. Of course, it was Norman who saw me first, his eyes widening slightly, but he didn't fully register what was happening until I stood behind Linda and faced the only unfamiliar face at the table.

"I'm guessing you're Linda's husband," I said, relishing the sudden silence. "I just wanted to wish you a happy birthday. I assume the pickle game went well?"

The man narrowed his eyes but responded in a cheerful tone. "Thanks! But it wasn't my birthday, and these guys bailed on me at the court, so we lost."

I tilted my head, glancing around the table.

"Sounds like a betrayal. What were they thinking?"

Norman shifted nervously, clearly wanting to speak, but Linda beat him to it.

"Margaret," she began, turning to face me. "I can explain. We—I was—"

Norman cleared his throat and interrupted her. "It was my idea... kind of. We had to figure out something. But we didn't want to drag you into it."

"It happened before you got here," Tara added quickly, her words tumbling out in a rush. Her forced smile and the way she avoided my gaze sent up a red flag. "We just need to fix it, that's all."

I crossed my arms and tried to keep my tone casual. "So, when you vandalized the department looking for a flash drive, that had nothing to do with me?"

Linda's eyes widened as she shook her head. "I didn't do that. Someone did break into—"

"You should tell her, Linda," her husband said firmly, squeezing her hand.

Linda sighed and looked down. "Before you started at the department, Troy asked me to clean his computer and save everything onto a flash drive. I didn't think much of it—all the projects were already on my computer. I thought maybe he had something private on there. Then, last Saturday, he called me late at night. He sounded upset—panicked, even. He asked about the flash drive, and when I told him it was on my desk, he... freaked out. I promised to grab it first thing in the morning, but when I got there... well, you saw the place. I looked everywhere—through the cabinets and files—but it was gone." She broke into tears, and her husband wrapped her in his arms.

"The flash drive wasn't there," Terry continued. "That's why I was under her desk. Linda told me about it, and we tried calling Troy, but we haven't been able to find him."

A pit formed in my stomach.

"We found the flash drive," I said, drawing everyone's attention. "Bruno found it near the pool."

Tara gasped, covering her mouth. The sound was sharp, almost theatrical, and I narrowed my eyes at her. "That's not good," she said, her voice trembling in a way that felt off. "We need to—I don't know, talk to someone—talk to Martin? He needs to know what's happening with the proposal."

"Are you crazy?" Terry cut in, panic lacing his voice. "Martin has to be in on it."

"He's not!" Tara snapped, her tone defensive and her reaction too quick. "Just like Troy, he was dragged into this, but he's not part of the fraud."

"Fraud?" I asked, though I wasn't entirely surprised. The mixed information and missing documents had already hinted at it.

Norman stood abruptly. "We need to talk to Logan—Detective Forest. He needs to know what's going on. This is already out of control."

I didn't mention what Logan had found by the pool or the content of Troy's email. Despite their nervousness, I believed them—they genuinely seemed concerned for a friend who might have made a bad choice.

"Mommy?" Darcy called from the shop, her face smeared with chocolate and a huge spoon in her hand.

"My daughter's waiting," I said, turning to leave. "It was nice to meet you, Mr. Linda's Husband."

Linda let out a soft chuckle as her husband stood and offered his hand.

"Bernard," he said. "Bernard Oak."

I shook his hand and gave them a reassuring smile. "I know this is a lot, but I'm with you. I want to figure this out as much as you do."

Flippers, Blades and Murder

Darcy greeted me at the counter with a suspicious paper bag in her hands.

Agnes winked at me. "We thought you might like some goodies for later."

Chapter 16

I had just sent Darcy to change into her pajamas when a soft knock at the door made my heart leap into my throat. I froze. It was late, and my mom had told me she was spending the night at my sister's house. She had her own set of keys.

The knock came again, followed by a soft bark. Relief flooded through me. I knew that bark.

When I opened the door, Logan stood on the other side, looking tired but determined.

"Did you come to arrest me or Darcy this time?" I asked, raising an eyebrow.

Behind me, a gasp made me turn. Darcy was peeking through the railing upstairs, her face full of curiosity.

"Come on, Maggie," Logan said with an

exaggerated sigh. "Now she's really going to think I'm scary."

He gave a small, crooked smile and raised an eyebrow at Darcy. "Which would be a problem because I wanted to ask her a favor."

I crossed my arms and glanced back at Darcy, who was creeping down the stairs, step by cautious step. Bruno, sitting by my side, wagged his tail furiously, the rhythmic thump of it against the floor echoing through the entryway.

"A favor?" I asked. "What kind of favor?"

Logan's expression softened. "It's for Darcy, so I hope we can talk?"

Darcy hesitated on the bottom step, half-hiding behind me. Bruno tilted his head, ears perking up at the sound of her name. Then, as if sensing she needed reassurance, he let out a low, friendly *whuff* and scooted a few inches closer to her, his tail still wagging wildly.

"Darcy," Logan said gently. "May I call you Darcy, or do you prefer Miss Willow?"

She clung to my hand but whispered, "Darcy is better."

Logan crouched to her level, his tone warm and reassuring. "Darcy, then. You see, I have a little problem. My partner here"—he motioned to Bruno—"needs someone to take care of him for a few days. He's a K9 officer, so he's kind of a big deal. But I thought maybe you could help me out."

Darcy tilted her head, frowning in confusion. "Who's Bruno?"

Logan chuckled and patted Bruno's head. "This guy right here. He's a real police officer, just like me. But he's got high standards, and I can't always keep up with them. Think you can?"

Bruno chose that moment to roll onto his back, his paws flopping into the air, and let out a little grunt. Darcy gasped and giggled, dropping to her knees to hug him. Bruno didn't hesitate, nuzzling into her belly and making her laugh even harder. When she stopped, he pawed at her hand gently, as if asking for more belly rubs.

If I'd thought ice cream was the ultimate way to light up my daughter's face, I'd been wrong. Darcy gasped again and giggled harder, now fully engrossed in scratching Bruno's ears.

"What?" Logan said innocently, shrugging at me.

"What?" I echoed, trying to keep my voice calm. I failed, though, because Darcy stopped playing and sat up, staring at me with wide eyes.

Flippers, Blades and Murder

"Is this okay, Mommy? I promise I'll take good care of him, and I won't let him pee all over Grandma's house."

I pressed my lips together, then gave her a tight smile. "Give me a second, sunflower."

I stepped outside with Logan, closing the door behind me. The moment we were alone, I smacked his arm.

"What were you thinking, bringing a dog to a five-year-old without asking me first? How am I supposed to say no now? Or explain the extra fur on my mom's couch?"

Logan's face grew serious, and his tone dropped. "I need you to keep Bruno here, Maggie. Like I told Darcy, he's an officer, and he'll protect you and your family."

A chill ran down my spine. "Why would I need protection?"

Logan hesitated, pacing the porch before speaking. "I found Troy."

I anticipated what was coming, and my heart sank.

"He was murdered," Logan said quietly.

I crossed my arms, hugging myself. "And you think I'm in danger?"

Logan exhaled sharply and rubbed his face. "I don't know. Right now, there's nothing pointing at you directly, but Maggie..." He paused, locking eyes with me. "You're the new director. I can't take that chance."

I sat down on the porch steps, my arms wrapped tightly around my knees. "I talked to Linda, Norman, Terry, and Tara tonight," I said quietly.

Logan sat beside me, waiting for me to continue.

"Troy called Linda last Saturday night. He was panicked and told her to keep a flash drive safe. She went to the office Sunday morning, but it had already been vandalized. She couldn't find it."

I hesitated, then forced myself to ask, "What happened to Troy?"

Logan looked away, his jaw tight. "Norman's skate."

I covered my mouth with my hand, horrified.

"We think it happened late last night or early this morning," Logan said. His fists clenched tightly, his knuckles white. "You told me he was missing, and I ignored it. I thought he was just being Troy—a pain. But I wish I'd listened. Maybe I could've stopped this."

I rested a hand on his shoulder. "I'm sorry. He was your friend."

Logan shrugged, his face a mask of guilt. "Not as good a friend as I should've been."

He stood abruptly, brushing off his jeans. "Keep Bruno close, Maggie. I know I told Darcy he's for her, but he's really for you. I have to head back to the station, but I'll check on you first thing in the morning."

I stood as well, nodding. "Does Bruno need food or anything?"

"He's already eaten, so don't let him fool you—he'll eat anything you give him. Just don't feed him from the table, and you'll be fine. Now, get inside. I'm not leaving until you lock the door."

I rolled my eyes but saluted playfully. "Got it."

As I turned to close the door, Logan stopped me.

"Tell your mom I'm sorry about the extra hair in her house," he said, his tone softening. "I just want to keep you safe."

I nodded, locking the door behind me. Bruno sat on the floor of the living room, where Darcy waited with a bright smile. He let out a huff and laid his chin on her lap, his tail wagging in steady thumps.

"Looks like you've got a new partner," I said to her.

But my mind was already racing with the weight of Logan's words.

I'd had a very long night, and my thoughts were scattered. Instead of heading to my office that morning, I waited until my mom came back to stay with Darcy and went straight to the police station. Though I wanted to leave Bruno to protect my family, I decided to follow Logan's advice for once.

The officer at the front desk was the same woman I'd met the night I'd come with my sister. She didn't wait for me to ask anything.

"He was waiting for you, but the chief just called him," she said, buzzing the door open and gesturing for me to enter. "Dr. Cooper wants to see you, though. You know his office, or Bruno here will lead you straight there." She smiled and gave Bruno a quick pat on the head.

"Dr. Cooper?" I asked, confused, until I remembered Arthur's last name. "You mean the ME's office?"

She nodded as if sending me to the morgue was perfectly normal.

I glanced around, trying to wrap my head

around where I was being sent. Across the room, I spotted an officer escorting Norman into an interview room. My heart sank. I knew why he was here, but his cheerful smile told me he didn't.

I tried to head toward him, to warn him, but Bruno had other plans. He tugged me toward the hallway, his leash taut as he led me to the stairs.

"Bruno, wait!" I whispered, but he was determined.

Reluctantly, I followed Bruno's lead down to the basement. This time, I had permission to be there, but somehow that made me feel worse.

As we reached Arthur's door, Bruno pulled harder, wagging his tail furiously before jumping up and pawing at it.

"Bruno!" I hissed, just as the door opened.

Arthur stood there, smiling as if he'd been expecting us. "Why am I not surprised to see you?" he said, scratching Bruno's ears.

Bruno ignored him and trotted inside like he owned the place.

"Hi," I said, feeling as confused as I sounded. "The officer at the front desk said to come here?"

Arthur grinned and tossed Bruno a treat.

"Do you think he's my most loyal visitor because of the treats, or does he actually like me? Don't answer—I'm happier pretending I'm his favorite."

I tilted my head, trying to stay on track. "Arthur—"

But he didn't let me finish. "Logan told me what's going on. I'm sure this isn't what you had in mind when you moved back to Apple Creek."

I sighed. "It's not, but Darcy loves it here." I shook my head. "I just wish this whole thing could be over."

Arthur's expression shifted. "I'm glad you're here early. I want to show you something."

A shiver ran down my spine. The last thing I wanted was to see a body. Still, my curiosity won out. Bruno, who had been attempting to open the treat jar on a cabinet, immediately trotted toward the morgue door.

"Seriously?" I muttered as I followed both him and Arthur inside.

I kept my eyes averted until I heard a loud thud. Turning, I saw Arthur standing by the autopsy table, a large black bag resting on it instead of a corpse.

Flippers, Blades and Murder

"This is Paul's hockey bag," Arthur said, donning latex gloves. "Don't touch anything."

"I wasn't planning on it," I replied, holding my hands behind my back.

Arthur opened the bag and pointed to a faint white residue along the zipper. "See this powder? It matches what we found on Hudson's body."

I leaned closer, noting the fine dusting. When I straightened, I spotted a whitish stain on the outside of the bag—similar to the one I'd seen near the Zamboni pit.

"What's that?"

Arthur grinned. "It's bleach powder. Lab tests confirmed it. My guess is the bag sat in a wet spot at the rink."

It clicked. Buckets of bleach powder had been in the rink during cleanups.

"Logan said Troy was murdered with another skate. Did you find anything in this bag?"

Arthur hesitated, his tone turning serious. "No powder in Norman's bag or on the skate Logan brought from the pool. But I did find it on the skate found by Troy's body. Here's the twist: Troy wasn't killed by the skate."

"What?" I blinked. "How did he die?"

"Chlorine gas exposure," Arthur said grimly. "A chemical weapon, originally used in

World War I. The blow to the head happened postmortem."

My stomach churned as I processed the horror of it. "Someone tried to frame Norman, didn't they?"

Arthur shrugged. "Could be. But I don't have a motive yet. That's Logan's problem."

"Motive..." I whispered, my mind piecing things together. The proposal, the construction, the missing invoices—it all led back to the flash drive. Someone was covering their tracks, trying to bury the evidence.

Suddenly, it hit me. "The buckets!" I exclaimed.

Arthur raised an eyebrow. "Buckets?"

Before I could explain, Bruno bolted to the office door, wagging his tail as Logan appeared.

"There you are," Logan said, petting Bruno's head. "You're so predictable."

He looked at me with a tired smile, his disheveled appearance betraying a sleepless night.

"Arthur fill you in?" he asked.

"I think so," I said, glancing at Arthur, who nodded proudly.

Logan's expression darkened. "I need to stop by the hospital to talk to Mrs. Taylor. Can you come with me? I could use your help understanding the department's procedures."

I hesitated, surprised by the invitation. Logan's stammering filled the silence. "I mean, if you're busy—your office—"

"No, it's fine," I interrupted, touched by his awkwardness. "This is more important."

Logan's shoulders relaxed. "Great. Let's go."

As I turned to thank Arthur, his knowing smirk stopped me.

"Good luck with the *files talk*," he teased.

I rolled my eyes and waved him off, ignoring the warmth creeping into my cheeks. I had bigger things to focus on—at least, that's what I told myself.

Chapter 17

"So the doctors believe she was poisoned?" I asked Logan as we approached Apple Creek General Hospital.

He gestured for me and Bruno to go first. "That's what the doctor told me. Mrs. Taylor inhaled a significant amount of chlorine gas. Fortunately, the exposure wasn't prolonged, so the damage was minor—well, aside from passing out and almost lung failure."

Logan called the elevator and lowered his voice. "Here's the thing. While the pool always smells like chlorine, I didn't notice anything unusually strong in her office. Bert didn't either."

I frowned, turning the idea over in my

head. "Did Bert say anything else? Do you think he could've done it?"

Logan shook his head. "Not a chance. Tara confirmed he was with her the entire time, and there's no way someone could've been exposed to chlorine gas and walked away unscathed. It has an immediate effect—eyes burning, throat closing. He wouldn't have been able to fake being fine."

"I'm not saying Bert did it, but..." I hesitated, noticing Logan's full attention locked on me. "What if Mrs. Taylor wasn't poisoned in her office? What if someone moved her there afterward? Then all the attacker had to do was leave before Bert showed up."

Logan pointed at me, a grin spreading across his face. "Exactly! That's what we're here to confirm with Mrs. Taylor." He stopped in front of a room and exhaled. "Not that I trust her. She's neck-deep in the fraud."

"Want me to play bad cop?"

He chuckled, shaking his head. "Maggie Willow, you're something else."

Without waiting for an answer, Logan knocked on the door and walked in.

"What's your problem?" Mrs. Taylor's voice cut through the room like nails on a chalkboard. She wasn't yelling at us, though. A nurse at her bedside rolled her eyes, clearly used to this behavior.

"Mrs. Taylor," Logan greeted her, his voice calm but firm.

She glared at us, her distaste palpable. "What do you want?"

"We need to ask you—"

"What you need to do is find whoever tried to kill me!" she snapped, attempting to sit up. The nurse firmly pushed her back onto the pillow.

"Hey!" Mrs. Taylor protested. "That hurts!"

The nurse bit her lip, shot us a look of pure sympathy, then mouthed, *Good luck,* before leaving the room.

Mrs. Taylor huffed. "I'll be filing a formal complaint about her. As for you," she fixed Logan with a glare, "I'm talking to your chief. He needs to hear about your utter incompetence on this case. Though, I suppose I see the problem." Her gaze shifted to me, sweeping me from head to toe with a look that could curdle milk.

Logan ignored her, but I couldn't. "What exactly are you implying? You're the one involved in fraud with the mayor and Hudson."

She bolted upright, her anger momentarily

overpowering her supposed injuries. "That's *Council Member Hudson* to you, young lady! My family isn't to blame for his murder. Or do you think I don't know about your brother-in-law? I'm sure it was your sister's idea—she's hated him since their school board days."

I took a step forward, but Bruno, sensing my temper, placed himself in front of me and rested his hand on my shoulder.

Logan didn't miss a beat. "How did you hear about Mr. Sullivan's involvement?"

Mrs. Taylor sniffed, her lips curling into a smirk. "I know plenty of people in this town. I practically *run* it."

Logan chuckled, shaking his head. "Really? Because two years ago, you didn't even live here. You moved in, started the swim club, and got cozy with the mayor. Convenient timing, wouldn't you say?"

Her arms crossed, but she leaned back, her bravado faltering.

"Tell me about the attack," Logan pressed.

Mrs. Taylor glanced out the window, her voice suddenly measured, almost rehearsed. "I was cleaning out my office for the bi-annual purge. I don't like clutter, so I moved files to the back storage. After my last trip, my nose started itching, my eyes watered, and my throat felt like it was closing. Next thing I know, I hit the floor. I must've struck my head because I passed out. I woke up here."

Logan nodded, stepping closer. "You think you hit your head, but the paramedics and doctors found no evidence of a concussion or head injury. How do you explain that?"

She hesitated. "Maybe I passed out from the gas."

"And you don't remember seeing anyone?"

"No, I was working alone."

Logan raised an eyebrow. "Maggie, how many people would you guess are interested in swimming in Apple Creek during summer?" He didn't wait for my answer, instead turning back to Mrs. Taylor. "So you're saying you packed all your files, carried them down the stairs, across the parking lot to the storage area, and back—all by yourself?"

She lifted her chin. "I'm strong and efficient."

"Impressive," Logan said dryly. "But not even a drop of sweat? You kept your sweatshirt on the whole time while hauling files in the heat?"

Her eyes widened, and she sputtered, "I—I don't get hot easily."

Logan slammed his palm on the bed rail, his voice rising. "Lying to a police officer is a crime, Mrs. Taylor. Obstruction of justice is another. Do you want to leave this hospital in cuffs?"

Her face paled, and for the first time, I saw real fear in her eyes. "I told you—I was moving—"

"Files," Logan interrupted. "We heard you. But either you weren't alone, or you weren't in your office. Which is it?"

She opened her mouth, closed it, and took a shaky breath. "The files were already in storage. I just needed something. They'd moved everything, and my office was useless."

Logan didn't back down. "Who's 'they'?"

She hesitated, her voice dropping to a whisper. "I don't know their names."

Logan's tone hardened. "Stop lying, Tonia. Who was cleaning up the pool construction with you?"

Tears spilled down her cheeks. "Raymond said we should focus on improving what we had since the proposal wasn't going anywhere. I didn't want the construction in the first place."

"Did someone attack you?" Logan asked.

"No, I decided to poison myself for fun!"

she snapped before glancing at me, her expression turning venomous. "What? You don't think someone could attack me?"

"Oh, I'm sure your *charm* wins people over," I said, unable to help myself.

Logan shot me a warning look before focusing back on Mrs. Taylor. "Tell me about the attack."

Her voice wavered. "Someone grabbed me from behind, dragged me into a closet, and slammed the door. I couldn't scream—my eyes burned, and the air tore at my throat. I passed out and woke up here."

Logan studied her for a long moment before delivering a chilling warning. "If I find out you lied about anything, I'll make sure you spend a long time behind bars."

Without waiting for a response, he opened the door and motioned for me and Bruno to follow him out.

As it happened, Logan wanted to discuss the proposal and the case, but not at the office. He drove us to Cider's Pub, Apple Creek's beloved tavern, claiming he desperately needed fish and chips.

"I can't believe you haven't been here since you got back, Maggie," he said as we slid into a booth. "This place is the reason I never left town."

I hesitated before speaking, my voice a little softer. "I would've thought this would be the last place you'd want to eat."

Logan glanced over the top of the menu, his expression softening despite the seriousness in his eyes. "Mr. Elliot's been a huge support for me. After he bought the place from my parents, he kept me on so I could pay for my training." He sighed, setting the menu down. "Sure, bad things happened, but..." He trailed off, forcing a chuckle as if brushing away the thought. "The food makes up for it."

I smiled faintly, turning to my own menu. My mom had told me how Logan's parents sold the tavern and moved to Florida after that strange spring break. The one where Logan and I had both almost ended up in jail.

"Can I ask you something?" I ventured, hoping I wasn't stepping over a line.

"Of course," Logan said, his tone shifting as he lowered the menu to meet my gaze. "You know you can ask me anything. I might not answer, though," he added with a teasing smirk.

I looked away, speaking softly. "How hard was it to change your life?"

His brow furrowed, and I tilted my head toward the room, silently explaining what I meant.

"I see," he sighed, leaning back. "After almost ending up in prison for something that happened right behind this place, nothing felt right. Was it hard to talk to my parents? Yeah. Were they upset? Probably. But..." He shrugged. "I couldn't live someone else's dream. Isn't that how you put it?"

I felt my cheeks burn, I forgot I said that. "I was just trying to help. You seemed lost... and sad. And, well, being charged with murder wasn't exactly helping. Is that why you became a detective?"

"Kind of," he said, tilting his head in thought. "After I stopped chasing my parents' dream, I was more lost than ever. I almost went to law school, but then..." He chuckled at some memory I couldn't see. "Chief Morales gave me the idea. We crossed paths again, but this time, I wasn't a suspect. He showed me how to channel everything into solving cases."

"Ben Morales? The guy who almost put you behind bars for life?"

"Exactly," Logan grinned, grabbing his menu again. "Though, to be fair, he wasn't leading that investigation, remember?"

Before I could respond, the waitress arrived with a wide smile. "Detective Forest! The usual?"

I chuckled as Logan launched into a playful exchange that ended with me being thoroughly convinced to order fish and chips—his usual, of course.

When the food arrived, Logan set down his fork, his tone shifting. "What do you think's really happening?"

I hesitated. Although I'd been obsessing over the murder and the proposal, I didn't have a clear answer. The night before, I'd used Darcy's little whiteboard to map out theories. After hours of scribbling and erasing, it was a tangled mess of possibilities.

"I'm really not sure," I admitted. "At first, I thought the murder was to cover up fraud, but now... I don't know."

Logan frowned thoughtfully. "Okay, let's try this. Walk me through how you'd handle it."

"The murder?" I asked, grinning as Logan choked on his drink.

"No!" he coughed, glaring as I tried not to laugh. "The proposal, Maggie. Focus."

"Right. Well," I said, composing myself, "you start with a reason for the project. There has to be demand—emails, complaints, suggestions, waitlists, things like that."

"So only residents can request it?"

"Not necessarily," I said, warming to the topic. "Other departments can approach us too. For example, if the police wanted to engage with youth, they might request outdoor courts in a specific neighborhood."

Logan raised an eyebrow. "Oddly specific."

I sighed. "Oh, yes. That one was a big deal in the city. Another way to initiate a project is if my department identifies a need based on enrollment numbers or demographics."

"So, do you think Troy fabricated the need for this project?"

I hesitated, aware of the tension in the question. "I really don't know. But if I decided we needed a new pool, I'd document the reasoning before presenting it to Martin and then the council, even if they rejected the idea."

Logan mulled this over as we ate in silence. Eventually, he set down his fork and leaned forward. "We've been combing through the flash drive, but aside from his last email, there's nothing about the proposal."

"It makes sense, though," I said.

He froze mid-bite. "Why?"

"Well, Troy left the department a year ago. He wasn't in charge of anything then. Norman was the acting director."

Logan frowned. "Who told you Troy left a year ago?"

I thought back. "When I interviewed with Martin, he mentioned the position had been vacant for a year. Why?"

Logan took a sip of his drink, his brow furrowing. "Troy wasn't gone. He was on sabbatical, working with the DNR on a wildlife project. Martin announced his resignation a month ago."

"Did you talk to Troy?"

Logan nodded. "Norman insisted on it. Losing Troy was an issue for the hockey league too."

"You played hockey with Norman?"

Logan smirked. "And Paul. We had to schedule different nights for obvious reasons."

I ignored the tangent, focusing on the case. "What did Troy say?"

"He confirmed the job offer and seemed

excited. That's why, when you told me he didn't reply to you, I wasn't too worried. The job required long stints in the wilderness."

I pushed my plate away, appetite gone. Logan noticed and reached out to touch my hand.

"Hey," he said gently. "I'll ask Martin why he lied. If he's hiding something, it's time to come clean. And for the record, R-Parks is lucky to have you."

I smiled despite myself, looking down to hide it. Logan leaned back, tossing a piece of fish to Bruno, who was curled up by my feet.

That's when it hit me. "Norman," I said.

Logan raised an eyebrow. "We've cleared him, Maggie. He and Paul were both framed."

"I know," I said quickly. "But Norman was working both jobs. The easiest way to manage would've been keeping all the paperwork in his office in the Operations and Maintenance building. That's why the records from a year ago are missing. Troy wouldn't have known when he asked Linda to wipe his computer."

Logan smacked the table. "That makes sense. Let's go. With any luck, Norman's still at the station."

Flippers, Blades and Murder

Chapter 18

Norman wasn't at the station anymore, but Martin was, and he wanted to talk to Logan. That left Bruno and me waiting outside the room. Instead of lingering, I decided to head back to the office—there was plenty to do.

The problem was, I couldn't concentrate on anything. My thoughts kept circling back to what we'd uncovered that morning.

Something about Mrs. Taylor's demeanor didn't sit right with me. I couldn't shake the feeling that she was hiding something. I felt bad for her, but I couldn't completely believe her.

"Hey, Maggie," Linda said, knocking on my office door. "I've got some papers that need your autograph, and can you clear these other folders so I can shred them? Some days I wish there was a simple way to get rid of all this information. Our shredder is incredibly slow!"

I waved her in, and she sat down in the chair across from me. Linda likely used keeping up with the office as a coping mechanism.

"About the birthday and the day off—"

"It's all right, Linda," I interrupted gently. "I understand you were just trying to help a friend."

Her eyes filled with tears, but she quickly composed herself. "He was such a nice person, Maggie. Only a monster would do this."

"I have to ask, Linda," I said, lowering my voice. "Did you ever notice anything strange going on around here?"

Her brows furrowed as she straightened in her chair. "Oh, absolutely. But not in our department—or so I thought."

"What do you mean?"

"Well, ever since we got this new mayor, little things haven't added up."

I leaned forward. "Little things?"

She nodded. "He never makes clear decisions. He's always asking for studies and proposals. That's why I didn't think much of this pool project. But..." She held up a finger. "The part about converting the ice rink? That part stayed hidden until the council meeting last month. I was shocked—people who use the rink were furious. That place is booked solid!"

"What other studies has he requested?"

Linda frowned. "You name it! He started with the Planning Department, looking for spaces to add new businesses. Then he turned his attention to us—sports, playgrounds, inclusion, aging, natural resources—you'd think he wanted a study on everything. But he never followed through or explained his plans."

"Sounds like a lot of extra work."

Linda nodded again. "And you know every study costs the residents money."

I felt my muscles tighten. "Do you have a list of all the studies and where the expenses went?"

"Sure. I can have it for you by tomorrow morning. But I can tell you now—all the expenses were taken from the outreach funding in the improvement budget."

"The outreach funding?"

Linda nodded. "The mayor and Councilmember Hudson both agreed to use that funding for the studies. They argued it was a way to 'engage with the community' by finding out what people were using or needed. It's a total scam, if you ask me."

I gave her a small smile of agreement, and she didn't need further prompting.

"I'll give you a copy of the budget and the expenses with the list," she said. Once I'd reviewed the files and signed the paperwork she'd brought, she left my office.

I glanced at Bruno, peacefully napping in a patch of sunlight near the window. The outreach funding was supposed to cover projects involving direct interaction with residents. Using it for studies wasn't unusual—unless you were overdoing it. I needed to find out who was leading all these studies.

"Can I interrupt?" Tara said, hesitating slightly as she stepped into my office.

"Please tell me nothing terrible happened—or that you're not quitting."

She laughed nervously. "Neither... kind of. Remember the community gardens by the reservation?"

"Of course. My mom used to rent one of those beds."

Tara scratched her head and glanced toward the door before meeting my eyes. "Well, we scheduled a truck to deliver organic fertilizer and supplies for gardeners starting late-season planting, but it got delayed. We sent an email, but some of the renters don't really check their inboxes." She sighed, clearly exasperated. "One person showed up this morning. Apparently, she found some kind of contamination in the bed openings and wants her money back. She's already complained to half the other renters."

"Who was it?"

Tara hesitated again, then spoke quickly. "Mrs. Williams. She owns the flower shop on Main Street."

"Gladys is still running the flower shop?"

"Do you know her?"

I nodded. "Oh, yes. My mom's good friends with her." I quickly added, "But I get it —she can be stubborn."

Tara shifted in her seat, her hands fidgeting in her lap. "Tell me about it. I told her we'd clean it up, but she insists we need to ensure the soil isn't contaminated. I'm telling you, Maggie, these gardeners are serious about their standards."

"I hear you. Some of them are meticulous about their soil's care. Did she say more about the contamination?"

"She said it looks like some kind of wet, light brown or beige mulch. I thought it might be mushrooms, but she wouldn't listen." Tara glanced down as if avoiding my gaze. "My solution is to offer refunds to anyone who asks, clean the affected beds, refill them, and leave them empty until next year. Otherwise, we'll get blamed for every bad tomato crop!"

I chuckled, about to agree, when it hit me. Linda thought our paper shredder was painfully slow, and that the city probably uses the same one in all its departments. Anyone trying to get rid of evidence fast would run into trouble. Another way to dispose of sensitive information was to dissolve papers with chemicals—like powdered bleach in large buckets.

"Light brown mulch?" I asked. "Does it smell like anything?"

Tara blinked, her fidgeting hands freezing mid-motion. "She didn't mention a smell, but—"

"It doesn't matter. I need to see this. Come on."

Tara looked startled, still sitting while I was already standing with Bruno's leash in hand.

"We can't let them cover it up!"

Montie Red

The fifteen-minute drive felt like forever. The community gardens were nestled just outside the lake reservation, a peaceful spot where my mom used to rent one of the gardening beds when Sandie and I were kids. We'd come over the weekends to check on our veggies. Honestly, it was a good thing we didn't depend on that harvest—we would have starved. But those weekends taught me how important these gardens were to some people.

Tara parked as close as she could, but there was still a short walk to the gardens. I practically speed-walked the entire way.

"Don't touch it!" I called out as soon as I spotted the fenced area that protected the gardens from hungry wildlife.

A man holding a rake froze mid-motion, his expression far from welcoming. Beside him stood Mrs. Williams, her arms crossed and her lips pressed into a tight line.

"Young lady," Mrs. Williams said sharply. "We paid for this gardening section, and I need to start planting now, or I won't have my Thanksgiving squash."

I stepped through the gate and onto the

soft soil, Bruno trotting beside me. He positioned himself between me and the Williamses, a quiet but unmistakable warning that made both of them take a cautious step back.

"Mrs. Williams, I understand," I said as I scanned the ground. "This won't take long—"

I stopped mid-sentence. The unmistakable tang of bleach hit my nose. Grabbing a nearby stick, I moved cautiously into the bed and poked at the damp soil.

"Hey!" Mr. Williams protested, taking a step forward. But Bruno's low growl was enough to make him freeze in place.

"Maggie, what are you doing?" Tara asked, standing at the edge of the gardening bed. Don't touch that mushroom or mold—it could be dangerous!"

I prodded a chunk of something white and soggy buried in the soil. It broke apart, revealing smaller pieces. Wet paper. My stomach tightened.

"Did you see any buckets around here?" I asked the Williamses, trying to keep my voice calm.

The irritation on Mrs. Williams's face gave way to unease. "No," she said slowly, her tone softening. Her eyes narrowed as she studied me. "Maggie? Are you Lucretia's girl?"

I gave her a quick smile. "Guilty as charged."

She shook her head, a faint smile tugging at the corners of her mouth. "You shouldn't be poking around on private property, you know."

"You wouldn't be the first person to tell me that this week," I said lightly. "But I'm the new R- Parks director, and you filed a complaint with our department this morning. So, we're here to help."

That seemed to please her. She turned to her husband and gave him a light smack on the arm. "See? I told you it was worth speaking up."

I let them be for the moment and turned to Tara. "We need to get the police here."

Tara blinked. "The police?"

I climbed out of the bed, wiping my hands on my jeans as I glanced around. "With any luck, we'll find the buckets somewhere around here."

"Buckets?" she repeated, her confusion growing.

But I was already walking, Bruno padding beside me as I began a slow circuit around the gardens, scanning for anything that didn't belong.

"Well," Logan said, walking toward Tara and me, "the forensics team will need to confirm it, but based on the smell, I'd say you're right—it's got some kind of chlorine in it."

I glanced back at the pitted holes in the ground. After checking all the beds, the police had confirmed that most of them contained the same strange mixture. Now it was up to me to figure out how to clean the soil and ensure it wasn't toxic before anyone planted anything.

"Any sign of the buckets?" I asked.

Logan frowned, his hands settling on his hips. "Nothing so far, but we need to review the security footage. I'm hoping we'll find something there."

"Security system?" Tara asked, her voice still tinged with shock. "I didn't even know we had one in the reservation."

Logan offered a small smile. "Technically, you don't. But we had reports of suspicious activity in this area a while back, so the chief decided to install cameras by the parking lot entrance and the park's main sections."

"Hopefully, there's something on the footage," I said, reaching down to pet Bruno, who sat dutifully by my side. "Maybe he can help?"

Logan chuckled, shaking his head. "The tricky part is I wouldn't even know what to ask Bruno to track. And..." He stepped a little closer, lowering his voice, "he doesn't exactly listen to me much yet. We're working on it."

Bruno tilted his head up at Logan, giving him a brief look of acknowledgment before returning his attention to the stick he was chewing on.

A loud crack of thunder made me glance at the sky. I hadn't noticed how dark the clouds had grown. A storm was rolling in fast, and the first gusts of cool wind sent a shiver through me.

"Why don't you two head back to City Hall?" Logan suggested. "This is going to take a while, and there's nothing else for you to do here."

Tara didn't hesitate. "That sounds great. I've got a ton of work waiting for me at the office."

"All right," I said, but before turning away, I faced Logan again. "Let me know if you find—"

Logan's expression turned serious, cutting me off. "Maggie, next time you decide to jump in and uncover incriminating evidence, *call me first*. I worry about you."

His tone caught me off guard, and I glanced down for a moment, feeling chastised. He wasn't wrong—I hadn't thought about the risks, only about preserving the evidence before someone destroyed it. And to be honest, I still wasn't sure how that strange mulch could prove anything.

"I brought an officer with me," I said, lifting one corner of my mouth in a half-hearted smile and pulling Bruno a little closer.

Logan exhaled, his expression softening. "Be careful, all right?"

I nodded, then turned and started walking back to the car with Bruno trotting beside me. Tara was already a few steps ahead, eager to leave.

As I opened the car door, the first drops of rain began to fall. I glanced back at Logan, still standing near the garden beds, his head tilted as if deep in thought. Despite his earlier frustration, I knew he only had my safety in mind.

Bruno hopped into the back seat, and as I slid into the driver's seat, I couldn't help but feel the weight of what lay ahead. Whoever had done this had gone to a lot of trouble to cover their tracks. And if we didn't find those

Montie Red

buckets—or a lead on the security footage—it was going to be nearly impossible to connect the dots.

For now, though, all I could do was hope the storm didn't wash away more than just the mulch.

Chapter 19

As I walked into the department, Linda stopped me by the door, her purse in hand and looking ready to leave.

"Margaret," she said. "I left the list you asked for on your desk, along with the papers I need you to sign before tomorrow."

I smiled at her. "I'll sign them right away and leave them in your—"

"Oh no," she interrupted, already halfway out the door. "Just leave them on your desk. Mine's still a mess."

I glanced at her desk and winced. She wasn't exaggerating—how she found room to write in that chaos was beyond me. "Have a nice evening!" I called after her.

Her muffled reply came just as the door closed behind her.

Terry strolled past me, chuckling. "She's always so particular on game days. Needs everything perfectly set before we hit the court."

"Pickleball?" I guessed.

Terry's grin widened. "Yep! We're reclaiming our championship at the high school tonight."

I waved him off, knowing how much pride the staff took in their games. It was endearing, even if it sounded a little over the top.

"He thinks too much of himself," Rufus said, striding toward the door. "With his coordination, it's a miracle he hasn't accidentally killed someone by losing his racket mid-swing."

"Paddle," I corrected, feeling my good mood slip away.

"Excuse me?" Rufus turned to give me the same disdainful up-and-down look his mother had perfected.

"Pickleball uses a paddle, not a racket," I said firmly. "And I don't appreciate your dismissive remarks about department employees."

He huffed, crossing his arms and glaring down at me. "Oh, really? And what are you going to do about it? You can't fire me. My mother owns—"

"Your mother owns what, exactly, Rufus?"

I asked, my tone icy. "Why don't you tell me what it is you think you own in Apple Creek?"

He rolled his eyes and tried to brush past me, but I stepped into his path.

"I'm serious. If I hear you bad-mouthing anyone else in this department, I'll make it my business to find out just how much your mother really owns in Apple Creek."

Anger flashed in his eyes as he stepped into my personal space, but I didn't back down.

"You don't want to mess with me, Margaret," he growled.

Before I could respond, Bruno lunged from the side. Rufus hit the ground hard, with Bruno towering over him, growling low and baring his teeth. Rufus's expression shifted from anger to sheer panic as he threw up his arms in a feeble attempt to shield himself.

"Get him off me!" Rufus screeched, his voice cracking. "He's going to kill me!"

Terry rushed back into the room, and I noticed Tara poking her head out of her office, her expression unreadable.

"Oh my goodness!" Terry exclaimed, looking alarmed. "We have to help him!"

I knelt beside Rufus, making sure he could see me. "I don't think Bruno appreciates your threats," I said, my voice calm.

I clapped my leg, and Bruno immediately backed off, though he stayed by my side, his sharp eyes locked on Rufus.

Rufus scooted backward until he hit a cubicle wall, then scrambled to his feet. "That beast shouldn't be in this office! He's a danger to society! I'll have him put down! He attacked me!"

Terry's face paled, but I caught a flicker of something on Tara's face—frustration? Anger?—before she disappeared back into her office.

Ignoring them, I turned back to Rufus. "Now you're threatening a police officer," I said, shaking my head. "Bruno might just arrest you."

Rufus's eyes darted between me and Bruno.

"He's what?"

"A K9 officer," I replied coolly. "I'm sure you know what that means, right?"

Rufus brushed off his suit and adjusted his tie, inching farther away from Bruno. "This isn't over, Margaret. I'm reporting this to the police."

"Great idea," I said, crossing my arms. "I'm sure they'll love hearing how one of their officers had to step in because you couldn't control yourself."

Flippers, Blades and Murder

Terry stifled a laugh as Rufus stormed out of the department.

"Are you okay?" Terry asked, turning to me.

"I'm fine," I said, managing a smile. "But you'd better get to your game. Linda will be mad if you're late."

He nodded, grinning, and hurried out. I turned toward Tara's office, but the door was already shut. Apparently, she was too busy to acknowledge what had just happened.

Just as Linda promised, I found the list on my desk—a five-page-long catalog of projects the mayor had requested. As I skimmed through the document, one detail stood out: "T.R." appeared next to most of the budget approvals. It made sense—Rufus Taylor had jurisdiction over those budgets—but I couldn't help wondering how well his department would function if all his funds went toward useless studies instead of actual projects.

Curious, I looked up Rufus's profile on the department website. Unsurprisingly, it offered no useful information. His social media, however, painted a different picture.

After scrolling through endless self-congratulatory posts, I found something useful from three weeks ago: a promise to his "supporters" that the Community Center would soon be "reclaimed," forcing those "useless" skaters to make do with a single ice sheet. I took a screenshot, along with the five comments—two from his mother—and moved on to her profile.

Her page was worse: full of defamatory posts about Community Center users and the R-Parks Department. According to her, having two ice sheets was a waste of space, and the city needed a new aquatic center. Yet there was no evidence she was qualified to teach swimming—or even knew how to swim. None of her photos showed her near a pool.

Frustrated by the lies, I took screenshots to share with the city lawyer. Then, on one of her older posts, I noticed a comment from two years ago by someone named Raymond H.: *"Now that I'm here, we'll take this to the finish line."*

Before I could look further, my phone rang. Councilmember Roberts's name lit up on the screen.

"Mrs. Willow," he said warmly. "I'm so glad I caught you."

"What can I do for you, Councilmember?" I asked, wary.

"Well," he began, "I'm trying to learn more

about this proposal the mayor and Hudson are so... determined to push. I want to help the city grow, of course, but I also want to save our residents from unnecessary taxes."

"I completely understand," I said. "I'm still working on gathering everything."

"I see. Well, it would be wonderful if you could stop by the Community Center's senior room and answer a few clarifying questions for us. It won't take long."

My heart sank. I knew it would take long, but I couldn't refuse. "I'll be right there."

"Excellent!" he said, sounding genuinely pleased. "We'll wait for you."

I glanced at my computer, debating whether five more minutes of research might reveal something crucial, but I knew it would only leave me more anxious.

After calling my mom to let her know I'd be late, I grabbed Linda's list and Bruno's leash.

"Come on, pal," I said. "Looks like we've got a long night ahead."

As I expected, the supposed short conversation stretched into at least two hours. It was interesting, though, and I had fun getting to know the senior leaders of Apple Creek. Council member Roberts was polite and understanding. Although some of his questions mirrored mine, he didn't get upset or defensive. Instead, he seemed genuinely eager to learn more about the R-Parks department.

The seniors were always a delightful group, especially when they defended me, the new member of the team, and playfully pressured Roberts to get the answers he'd been avoiding.

But as much fun as I had, I was ready to go home. It had been a long day, and through the roof, I could hear the pouring rain and rumbling thunder. I wanted to be with Darcy. She was still scared of storms.

"Let's go, Bruno," I said, and my furry friend happily trotted by my side.

Everyone had gone home by the time we walked down the hallway. I was thankful to have Bruno with me, especially when we passed the doors to the ice rink and noticed the yellow tape still on the ground. My heart raced, and I stopped a few steps away from the door.

From where I stood, I could see the main entrance. A flash of lightning illuminated the entire lobby and part of the parking lot, revealing the torrential rain outside. Aside from the rhythmic sound of the water, everything was eerily quiet. I exhaled, shaking my head. I wasn't even sure if the ice rink was still considered a crime scene. For all I knew, the police had just forgotten to remove the tape.

I took a step forward, but the light from the lobby flickered. It looked more like the beam of a flashlight. At my side, Bruno froze, his fur bristling as he let out a low growl.

Logan's words echoed in my head. I didn't hesitate this time. I pulled out my phone, mentally noting to save his number on speed dial, and quickly searched for his contact. Maybe I should've called 911, but I wasn't thinking about my own safety as much as the fact that someone was trespassing in a crime scene.

"Hi, Maggie," Logan's voice came through. "I hope you're not mad. What Martin had to say was interesting. Apparently, Troy quit, but told Martin to keep it under wraps until his DNR work was done. Anyway, I'll fill you in—"

"Someone's in the ice rink," I whispered, stepping back from the rink's doors.

"Maggie, is Bruno with you?" he asked, his tone now serious.

"Yes."

"Can you get out of there safely?"

Montie Red

I turned toward the main entrance. Without the lightning, it was hard to see much. "I think I can make it to my car."

"Good," he said, his voice tense. At the same moment, lightning illuminated a dark SUV parked in the front lot. "Don't hang up. Walk to your car. I'm on my—"

Before he could finish, or I could respond, a hand grabbed my shoulder. The grip was so tight it sent a sharp pain all the way down my arm. My phone slipped from my hand.

Bruno surged forward, his body slamming into whoever was behind me. This time, he didn't just growl—he bit. I heard the dreadful sound of teeth sinking into flesh, followed by a man's scream.

"Stop!" the man shouted, but his grip loosened, and I felt him release me.

Outside the main entrance, I caught the shape of someone approaching, though I couldn't make out who it was. A flashlight rolled at my feet, and I realized the man behind me must have come from the rink. With no other option left, I hoped that meant the rink was empty, and I rushed through the doors into the darkened and cold arena.

Flippers, Blades and Murder

The cold of the rink hit me as soon as I stepped inside, along with the suffocating darkness. The rain pounding on the roof drowned out most sounds, making it impossible to tell if someone else was here or if the men had followed me. My chest tightened as I silently cursed myself for not waiting for Bruno.

My foot struck something large on the floor, and I barely had time to throw my hands up to stop myself from falling. I stumbled forward, only to bump into the metal cage under the stands where we stored the rental skates and skating school equipment. I leaned back against it, closing my eyes for a moment, forcing them to adjust to the dimness.

When I opened them again, shadows slowly took shape. A hockey bag lay in the middle of the floor, its contents scattered across the mat. My breath hitched when I realized there was only one skate.

"Check that side," a man's voice barked, echoing off the walls. It sounded familiar, but the rain and the cavernous rink distorted it. I didn't hear a response. Worse, there was still no sign of Bruno.

Staying low, I crawled along the hall, keeping close to the metal cage. If I could make it to the back of the rink, I could slip out through the Zamboni doors. I was halfway there when a bulky shape caught my eye. Lightning illuminated the rink, briefly casting a blade's metallic gleam across the floor. I bit back a scream as thunder rolled through, shaking the stands.

I hurried toward the shape, my stomach sinking when I found Martin's unconscious body. My heart pounded as I knelt closer, relief washing over me when I saw he was still breathing—though barely.

Then I heard it: the Zamboni door rolling open, its heavy groan muffling the rain.

"This is a nice turn of events," a woman's voice called behind me, sharp and cold. "And before you get any ideas, we locked the rink entrance. Your ridiculous dog won't be helping you anymore."

My blood ran cold as recognition hit me like a brick. I turned slowly, my mind racing. The initials on the list weren't for "Taylor Rufus"; they were for "Tara and Rufus." Rufus, the man who'd tried to grab me in the lobby, was now driving the Zamboni. That explained why Bruno had attacked him—he'd sensed the danger. And Tara's earlier unease? She must've been panicking over what I'd uncovered in the garden beds.

"I thought you liked Martin," I said, forcing myself to meet her gaze even as I instinctively stepped back.

She tilted her head, eyeing Martin's labored breaths. "He was all right. Made it easy for him to believe I really needed his help tonight. No questions about the Community Center or why it had to be so late. But he shouldn't have betrayed me."

"Betrayed you?" My voice rose. "You killed two people!"

"I didn't kill anyone," she said with a sigh, as if I were being unreasonable. "But I guess now you'll never hear the news. Next week, the mayor will be found guilty of this conspiracy."

I stepped back again, bumping into Martin's legs. Tara laughed.

"You know this is all his fault," she said, pointing at Martin. "He wasn't supposed to hire anyone to fill Troy's job. That position was Rufus's by right."

The Zamboni engine shut off, plunging the rink into an eerie silence. The steady drum of rain on the roof seemed louder now.

"Hey," Tara shouted, her voice echoing. "I

found her. I guess we can wrap this up tonight. You know, two stones, one bird."

I shook my head, slipping my hand behind me until my fingers brushed against the laces of the skate. My stomach churned as I slowly pulled it free. It was reckless—I knew I shouldn't touch a potential murder weapon—but I had no option.

"It's 'two birds, one stone,'" I said.

Tara's brow furrowed as she turned toward me. "Really? You want to correct me before I kill you?"

"I'd rather not get killed, but that was ridiculous!"

She leaned closer, her sneer sharp as a knife. That was all the opening I needed. I gripped the skate blade tightly and swung it at her head. She stumbled back, clutching her temple as she fell to the floor. I didn't wait to see if she'd recover—I bolted.

Ideally, I'd have opened the Zamboni storage room door and driven out, but the glass doors blocked the rink's corridor. I didn't want to test Tara's warning about the front entrance being locked. My only hope was to distract Rufus and hope he took the bait.

"Tara?" Rufus's voice boomed from the direction of the door I needed.

Flippers, Blades and Murder

I grabbed a puck from the hockey bag and sprinted toward the stands, staying low in the darkness. I hurled the puck in the opposite direction. It clattered loudly, its echoes bouncing off the walls. Rufus cursed and started climbing the stands, chasing the noise.

I darted onto the ice, my feet sliding as I struggled to find balance.

"She's on the ice!" Tara shrieked.

I didn't dare look back but heard Rufus's heavy footsteps as he stomped down the stands. I tried to run-slide across the ice, but I didn't want to fall. If I did, he'd catch me for sure.

"I'm going to—" Rufus started to shout. The loud thud that followed, along with a string of curses, told me he'd slipped.

I pushed myself harder, ignoring my pounding heartbeat and the growing panic. My feet hit the first mat near the storage room just as Rufus grabbed my foot, yanking me down. I kicked back, my shoe connecting with his face. He swore again, but I didn't care. I scrambled forward, crawling and pulling myself as fast as I could.

I reached the door, my hand on the knob, but Rufus's voice stopped me.

"It doesn't matter if you get out," he

sneered. "You know I'll outrun you... or I'll visit your home later."

I didn't know if he was right, but I wasn't about to find out. My mind raced with thoughts of Darcy and my mom. There was no way I was putting their lives in danger. I looked around, and then I understood their plan.

"You bleached the paper trail here," I said, pointing at the pit while watching him wipe his mouth. "And you used the bleach powder buckets to dispose of the mixture. Burying it was your best option. That's why Tara was so upset about closing all the programs."

"It was a smart move, until useless Harold saw the buckets outside," he said, standing just off the ice, a smug smile on his face. "But please, I'd love to hear how much you've figured out. It's always a nice surprise to bump into smart people."

I scanned the storage room and froze when I spotted one of the bleach powder buckets. Of course, they needed one—it was used to dispose of more evidence. The one I'd just found. I turned and saw a couple of boxes with the swimming club logo on them.

"Oh, you see it," Rufus said, his voice tinged with pride. "You were getting too close, Maggie. Time to shut this down."

"Your mom?" I asked, not fully believing what I was hearing.

He shook his head and raised his voice. "She's the one who complicated everything! Who do you think killed Hudson?"

My expression must have been obvious, because he laughed and added, "The idiot told her he was out and even threatened her with destroying her beloved nonprofit if she tried to involve him with the rink."

"Because it would be a hit to the Community Center, and she needed to make a point. To prove she really owns Apple Creek," I dared to say, which made Rufus smile.

"Exactly!"

"But you poisoned her!"

He shrugged. "I didn't want to, but she insisted. According to her, it would be too suspicious if nothing happened with the pool part of the deal. Especially with the mayor so against it."

I tried to absorb what he was saying as I backed into the storage room. A plan started to form in my head.

"You purposely poisoned your mother?"

"As if you've never wished harm on someone before," he mocked.

I shook my head.

"Let's be done with this," he said.

I spotted the bleach powder bucket near the wall. Acting quickly, I kicked it over, spilling its contents. As Rufus hesitated, I grabbed a cleaning bottle and hurled it into the powder. A greenish smoke began rising immediately, filling the storage room.

My eyes stung as I held my breath, fumbling for the door. Behind me, Rufus coughed and cursed as he stumbled. I didn't wait—I shoved the door open and ran.

The rain hit me like a wave, but it was the flashing red and blue lights of the patrol cars that stopped me.

"Maggie!" Logan's voice called out. I felt a hand grab my arm, steadying me just as Rufus burst from the rink.

Bruno leaped at him, his powerful jaws clamping down on Rufus's arm and forcing him to the ground. Rufus howled in pain, thrashing under Bruno's weight.

Logan pulled me back as green smoke billowed from the rink's storage room, mingling with the rain as sirens wailed in the distance.

Chapter 20

The rain had stopped what felt like an eternity ago, but I remained wrapped in a thick blanket on the back of an ambulance. Twice in one week, I'd ended up in this peculiar position. How? At least now I understood Bert's reluctance to give up the blanket—it felt like the safest place in the world.

"It looks like the smoke didn't spread too deep into the rink," Logan said as he approached. "Still, I'd rather close the Community Center for at least a day, just to be safe."

I nodded, though my mind was elsewhere.

"How's Martin?" I asked, holding my breath.

"The ambulance just got him to the hospital. We'll know more soon, but..." Logan sat beside me, his voice softening. "The paramedics were optimistic. You saved his life, Maggie."

I dropped my gaze and closed my eyes. "I forgot he was in the rink when I knocked over that bottle of bleach. I could have killed him. Like Troy."

Logan gently turned me by the shoulders until I faced him.

"You caught two killers and saved a man's life. That's what happened, Maggie."

Tears welled in my eyes, and my voice cracked. "But my fingerprints are on the skate, Logan."

To my surprise, he laughed quietly, pulling me into a hug.

"Margaret Willow," he murmured near my ear, "you are something else."

Over his shoulder, I saw two officers escorting Tara and Rufus, both in handcuffs, to waiting patrol cars. Logan must have sensed my unease because he glanced back.

"Did you get their story?" I asked.

"Oh, yes," he said. "Didn't take long for Rufus to throw Tara under the bus."

I straightened. "Did you figure out Mrs. Taylor's connection to Hudson?" I didn't wait for him to answer. "I think she cheated to get him elected, and he was returning the favor. Then I came along, and the residents started to see him as the council member who constantly fought with the mayor. I guess he figured he'd repaid his debt to her."

Logan smiled. "Of course, you'd figure that out. Rufus wanted to be the R-Parks Director to control the budgets. He promised Tara a promotion—with more programs and a pay raise—if she helped. Hudson approved everything, but things unraveled when Troy found the paper trail."

"Was it on Norman's computer?"

"Exactly. Norman had no idea, but when he moved Troy's files into his office, he accidentally copied the evidence of Hudson and Rufus's communications."

"So, where did all the money go?"

Logan arched an eyebrow and nodded toward the patrol car where Rufus was being shoved inside. "Mrs. Taylor's nonprofit received several large donations over the past year—all from a shell company called H & Jones. Suspiciously, the money flow stopped about a month ago, right when Martin announced the opening for Troy's job. We'll interrogate Mrs. Taylor, but I believe Rufus when he says Hudson underestimated her. That woman's thirst for power and money drove her to do anything—including killing Hudson when he became inconvenient."

A shiver ran down my spine. She had threatened me too.

Logan continued, "After Hudson's death, they had to clean up the mess. It makes sense that he wanted out—he must have realized it was too risky to keep their scheme going with someone new in charge."

"Someone not involved in their scam," I murmured.

"Exactly. One of Troy's files included an agreement between Hudson, Troy, and Mrs. Taylor. Hudson used it as leverage to keep them quiet. But the mayor—" Logan hesitated, his tone softening. "He was innocent, Maggie. Turns out, he was the one feeding Troy evidence. He must've known Hudson was dirty and wanted to expose him but couldn't do it directly. The mayor only wanted to protect the city."

The patrol cars drove off, their red and blue lights fading into the rain-soaked night.

"Money and politics," I said, shaking my head. "Never a good combination."

Logan nodded, and I leaned on his shoulder.

"I should call my mom—"

Logan tensed beside me. "She's going to hate me even more, isn't she?"

"She doesn't hate you!"

He didn't reply, just offered me his hand to help me down from the ambulance. "Come on. I'll drive you home. It's late."

Bruno hopped up beside me, his tail wagging like a helicopter blade as his big brown eyes locked onto mine. I crouched to pet him, running my fingers through his thick fur and scratching behind his ears. He leaned into my touch, his tail thumping against the ambulance step.

"I'm so glad you're okay," I whispered, pressing my forehead against his. He let out a happy little grunt, his tongue darting out to give my chin a quick lick.

"He's the one who led us to the back of the rink," Logan said, leaning down to give Bruno a quick scratch behind the ears. "When I got to the rink and couldn't open the ice arena's door, Bruno bolted outside and circled the building. He didn't hesitate—he knew exactly where you were."

I wrapped my arms around Bruno, burying my face in his fur. He let out a soft, contented whine and nuzzled against me, his wet nose pressing into my shoulder. Then he shifted his weight slightly, resting his big paw on my leg as if to reassure me everything was okay now.

"You're my hero, Bruno," I murmured, holding him close.

"Logan?" I said, using my sweetest tone.

"Yes, Maggie?" he replied, suspicious.

"Can Bruno stay with me tonight? I know the danger is gone, but... my mom's going to be mad, and Darcy will be devastated if she doesn't get to say goodbye to him."

Logan threw up his hands, shaking his head as he walked to his car. But I caught the faint smile tugging at his lips.

Bruno seemed to understand and approve of my request. He licked my face and leaned into me so hard I nearly fell backward.

"Just like I told you before, you bring nothing but trouble into this house!" Mom's voice rang out as I stepped in from the backyard. "What are you thinking?"

I froze, halfway through the door, as her words hit me.

Before I could answer, I heard his voice.

"I understand, Mrs. Willow," Logan said from the porch, his tone calm but tinged with urgency. "But you have to believe me. I had no intention to—"

Mom stood just inside the doorframe, arms crossed. I slipped in behind her, catching sight of Logan, who lingered on the porch, careful not to crowd her.

"Mom," I said gently, placing a hand on her shoulder. "We've already talked about this. Logan didn't do anything wrong, and I'm okay."

She turned her head just enough to shoot me a pointed look, the kind that said she didn't appreciate the interruption.

"I wasn't even talking about that, Margaret," she snapped, then turned back to Logan and jabbed a finger in his direction. "This gentleman had the audacity to bring a dog into my house, disrupt my peace, and now expects us to just give him back? I'm not having it. Not again. You know what this will do to Darcy."

I glanced inside, where Darcy was busy showing Bruno a treat. From the way she gestured, I guessed she was trying to train him to navigate some imaginary obstacle course.

"That wasn't—" Logan began, his voice

faltering slightly. "That isn't my intention. I was only thinking about Maggie's safety."

When Logan had left Bruno with us that night, I'd anticipated Darcy would have a hard time letting him go. What I hadn't expected was my mom's sudden attachment to him. Although I should have, considering Bruno had a strong connection with Ben, the man I suspected she was still in love with. Over the past two days, we'd had more than one conversation about it.

"Mom, we've talked about this," I said. "Bruno isn't a pet. He's a police officer."

Mom planted her hands on her hips and raised an eyebrow. "Oh, really? Because this is *exactly* how all officers behave at the station."

I followed her gaze to Bruno, who was sprawled out on the floor, belly up, while Darcy scratched his stomach. His tongue lolled out of his mouth, and one of his legs twitched in delight.

"He's undercover?" I joked, laughing at myself. Logan's quiet chuckle eased some of the tension, but Mom's stern expression didn't waver.

"I'm not giving him back," she declared, her voice softening as she turned to Logan. "I'm not ungrateful, Detective. I can't tell you how much I—" Her voice caught, and she took a moment to compose herself. I wrapped my arm around hers and leaned closer for support.

"Thank you for saving my baby," she continued, her voice trembling. "I heard Bruno did most of the work, but it was your idea to protect my Maggie. And I'm keeping him."

She gave my hand a squeeze before walking into the house. I watched as she joined Darcy and gave Bruno a firm scratch behind the ears before calling them both into the kitchen.

"I thought you said she was going to hate having dog hair in the house," Logan said.

I shook my head, smiling. "I didn't see this one coming."

Logan leaned against the porch railing, crossing his arms. "Here's the thing, Maggie. If you're okay with it, I'd really like you to keep Bruno."

"You too?" I asked, raising an eyebrow.

"Long story short?" He didn't wait for me to answer. "Ever since Chief Morales retired and left Bruno with me, he hasn't been himself. You've seen him—he doesn't listen, he's always running around the station, playing with everyone. It's like he's searching for something."

"Funny," I said, frowning. "Because that sounds exactly like how he always behaves."

Logan laughed, shaking his head. "Maybe. But when he's with you, he's different. He's happy. And honestly, the thought of him going back to my place, lying around watching bad TV with me..."

"Bad TV?"

"Sports," he admitted with a sheepish grin. "My teams are always losing."

I chuckled, crossing my arms. A month ago, I wouldn't have believed this conversation would ever happen—me standing on my mom's porch, talking about dogs and bad TV with Logan.

"Well," I said, tilting my head, "I think Mom might forgive you if she gets custody of Bruno."

Before Logan could reply, Darcy peeked around the doorframe, her small face full of curiosity.

"Well, hello, Miss Willow," Logan said, crouching down. "What's the plan for today?"

Darcy hesitated, looking at me before stepping onto the porch. "Are you taking Bruno back to your house?"

Logan smiled. "Actually, I was just telling your mom that Bruno seems happier here—

with you and your grandma. He told me so himself."

Darcy fidgeted with her fingers. "But... what if you miss him? Won't you be all alone?"

Logan's laughter was soft and warm. "You sound just like your mom," he said with a warm smile. Then, as his gaze flicked to mine, my heart skipped a beat. "But Bruno didn't live with me before. He used to live with a friend who moved away. I don't think he was very happy with me. And honestly, I'd rather see him here, where he's happy. Plus, I will see him at work when your mom drops him at the station."

"Oh, will I?"

He winked at me, but Darcy's face lit up and got all my attention. "So we can keep him?"

I nodded. "I think so. Otherwise, Grandma would never forgive me."

Darcy squealed with delight and threw herself at Logan, wrapping her arms around his neck.

"Thank you! Thank you! Thank you!" she shouted before running back inside. "Grandma! We're keeping Bruno!"

Logan stood, brushing off his knees. "That went better than expected."

"Well, you did just give her a puppy," I teased.

"I had a different plan for this morning, actually," Logan confessed, scratching the back of his neck.

"Oh?"

"I thought Darcy would be heartbroken, and I was going to take you both out for dessert to make up for it. But since your mom has other plans, maybe you'd like to join me later?"

"We haven't had lunch yet," I pointed out, enjoying the way his shoulders slumped in mock defeat.

"Okay, fair. How about I meet you after lunch?"

"Or," I said with a grin, "you could stay for lunch and we all go for dessert together."

Logan hesitated, glancing toward the house. "Maggie, I haven't been in your mom's house since that spring break. I don't think she'll—"

"Mom!" I called, cutting him off.

She poked her head out of the kitchen.

"Got room for another plate?"

Mom looked surprised, but then a knowing smile crept onto her face. "Of course. Though I'm worried I didn't make enough. I remember that boy's appetite for fish fry."

Logan's eyes widened in alarm. "Fish fry?" he mouthed.

I laughed, gesturing for him to step inside. "After you, Detective Forest."

Bruno raced past us, wagging his tail so hard his entire body wiggled.

As I followed Logan into the house, I couldn't help but smile. Watching Darcy climb onto a stool, Mom set the table with a plate of golden, homemade fried food, and Logan joining us, I realized I'd found my way home.

Bruno nudged my leg, and I bent down to scratch behind his ears. "Come on, buddy," I murmured, scratching his ears. "This is home now."

Epilogue

"**M**argaret!" Martin's voice boomed across the lobby as soon as I set foot inside City Hall a week after the chaos unfolded.

"Hey!" I called back, walking toward him with Bruno at my side. "How are you feeling? I thought you'd be out of the office for at least another week."

Martin made his way over slowly, his steps measured, and though he smiled, there was a sadness in his expression that made my heart ache. He looked pale and thinner than before. I didn't know how deep his relationship with Tara had been, but being used and nearly killed by someone he cared about couldn't be easy to recover from.

"I needed the distraction," he admitted,

crouching slightly to pet Bruno's ears. "And I heard this guy has a new address. How's he settling in?"

He seemed eager to shift the conversation, and I was happy to oblige.

"It's going great. He keeps the family busy every evening, and he gets me up early every morning."

Martin chuckled, his first genuine laugh. "Well, I won't complain about that—especially with what's coming up in the next few weeks."

I blinked, confused. "The next few weeks? What do you mean?"

"The art festival?" he said, his brows knitting together. When I didn't respond, he sighed and crossed his arms. "Margaret, you live here. It's one of the biggest events in the city. Please don't tell me Tara—oh no. Of course. You haven't gotten anything about it yet because we don't have a Recreation Program Manager."

He shook his head, muttering to himself in mock exasperation. His attempt at humor didn't ease my growing sense of dread.

"It'll be fine," he added, as if trying to convince himself. "Linda and Terry should be able to get you up to speed. The only person to watch out for is Mrs. Roberts."

"Who's Mrs. Roberts?" I asked, suspicion creeping into my voice.

Martin cleared his throat and shifted awkwardly, as though he was ready to bolt. "Well, she's Councilmember Roberts' wife and also happens to be the President of the Art Festival Committee. I'm sure you'll meet her soon enough."

"Martin!" I shouted, just as he reached the elevator and pressed the button, clearly hoping to escape. "How—when is this festival? I don't know anything about it! I barely remember my mom taking me when I was a kid!"

"See? You remember! And don't worry—you've got, what? Three or four weeks to get it done?"

The elevator doors opened, and Martin stepped inside but held them open, flashing me an apologetic smile. "You'll do great, Margaret. I believe in you. And, uh, if you need anything, please come to my office. I'd rather not set foot in the R-Parks department for a while."

Before I could protest, the doors slid shut, leaving me standing in the middle of the lobby with too many questions, an overwhelming sense of urgency, and a newly developing fear of Mrs. Roberts.

"Come on, Bruno," I said, giving his leash a

gentle tug as we headed toward the police station. "Hopefully your day will be less strange than mine has been so far."

I hope you enjoy the first installment of Apple Creek R-Parks Department Mysteries and are excited to read the next book; **Festivals, Art and Poison.**

As I sat on a bench in the museum's lobby, I kept wondering how I, once again, found myself surrounded by the police department, crime scene tapes and a body in a room too close for my comfort. I wanted to call my mom and tell her the reason I wasn't at home, but I doubted it was a good idea. By now, she must have met with Ben and I didn't know how that went. So, I called Sandie and briefly told her something had come up at the museum.

"Margaret," police officer Tricia Green

approached me with a notebook in hand. "Can I take your statement?"

I stood up and followed her to the office at the main level of the mansion. I was glad to see her and not Deputy Warren, the one I had to talk to. It may be unfair since I had never met the man, but between Logan's warning and the way he reminded me of Officer Collins, the corrupted one who tried to frame Logan and me years ago, I didn't trust him.

"Do you want to begin by explaining your reason for being in the museum after hours?" Tricia said, in an almost apologetic tone.

If you want to learn what happened between Maggie and Logan back on that Spring break, get your free prequel here.

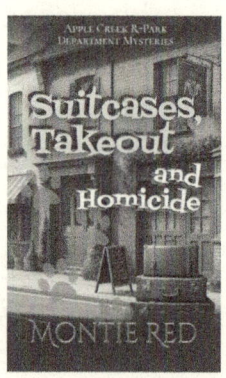

Acknowledgments

For your patience, support, belief in the cause, staying with me and tolerating the time that I took away from all of you to sit down and write. During these years, I learned so much from all of you. For listening to my stories, complaints, and successes. For your help and critiques, for all of these and more,

To Each one of you, who loves to read mysteries and took the time to read my take on them. My amazing coaches; Scarlett and Bryan, my mystery group friends, Mom, Gloria, Teddy, Josephine, and You up there...

Thank you.

About the Author

Hi, I'm Montie Red, and I have a not-so-secret addiction to crafting twists, turns, and mysteries best solved with a cup of tea (or maybe a snack). My *R-Parks Mysteries* series is inspired by my love for quirky small-town charm, meddling sleuths, and the occasional murder that needs unraveling—purely fictional ones, of course!

My biggest motivation is my amazing daughter, who keeps me inspired and grounded. We share our home with two lovable dogs, five chatty birds, and a husband who frequently attempts daring escapes from my writing world—usually by pretending there's a very important game to watch or a mandatory tee time.

When I'm not diving into cozy mysteries, I step through portals to other worlds, writing sci-fi and fantasy adventures under the pen name Monica Red. Whether it's catching a killer or navigating interstellar chaos, I'm always in the thick of an exciting tale.

Thanks for joining me on this storytelling journey. Grab a cozy blanket, dive into a book, and let's solve some mysteries together!

Made in United States
North Haven, CT
20 July 2025